"I shouldn't have kissed you," she said softly

Geoff felt Petra starting to stand up, and he reached for her. "Why shouldn't you have?" he asked. "I liked it."

"And I liked it, too...and the feel of you, but—"

Geoff sensed her trembling as he pulled her into his arms.

"Geoff, I don't think we should get involved. It would be too dangerous."

"Dangerous?"

"Geoff, I have to swim that lake. I can't let anything get between me and the—the swim. If I got more... involved with you—"

His arms tightened around her. "You can say it, Petra, it won't burn your tongue."

"If I slept with you, then I would be thinking about you. I'd lose my ability to concentrate. I can't afford that, Geoff." She slipped out from his arms, knowing she couldn't reveal her deeper fears.

CLAIRE HARRISON works hard at writing and loves it. After all, she says, hers is one of the few professions that allows one to earn a living, have a choice of heroes and play God with hundreds of characters. Now that her husband, a scientist, is no longer posted in Washington, she and her family make their home in Canada.

Books by Claire Harrison

HARLEQUIN PRESENTS

These books may be available at your local bookseller.

Don't miss any of our special offers. Write to us at the following address for information on our newest releases.

Harlequin Reader Service
901 Fuhrmann Blvd., P.O. Box 1397, Buffalo, NY 14240
Canadian address: P.O. Box 603,
Fort Erie, Ont. L2A 9Z9

CLAIRE HARRISON

love is a distant shore

Harlequin Books

TORONTO • NEW YORK • LONDON
AMSTERDAM • PARIS • SYDNEY • HAMBURG
STOCKHOLM • ATHENS • TOKYO • MILAN

This book is dedicated to
Mary Connell of Whitby, Ontario,
whose graceful title adorns its cover
and who helped me understand
that a swim like Petra's can change people.

Harlequin Presents first edition November 1986
ISBN 0-373-10930-X

Original hardcover edition published in 1986
by Mills & Boon Limited

CHAPTER ONE

GEOFFREY HAMILTON sat on the bench, shifted his aching leg slightly and glared down at the figure in the pool below. He would have liked to curse out loud, but his mother had brought him up to be a damned gentleman and, somewhere along in his wayward youth, he'd managed to absorb enough of her teaching to know that it wasn't proper to swear in the presence of a lady, even if she was immersed in water and seemingly oblivious of his existence.

Still, nothing stopped him from having his own private thoughts, and those were dark, gloomy and angry. He wondered what the hell he was doing, sitting in a pool in Toronto and watching a skinny little number like Petra Morgan make her 100th lap of the pool and acting as if it were her first. Back and forth, back and forth, arms going around in that perfect front crawl. Up, around and over. Up, around and over. Swim to the end, tuck and curl, shoot out into the water again. And, all the while, her coach, Joseph McGinnis, was pacing beside her, looking smug and shouting the occasional encouragement in her direction. As if she needed it. Geoff didn't think he'd ever seen anyone with a mind on such a single track as Petra Morgan.

He could have killed his boss, Rick, who had conspired to put him on this beat. If he'd known what was in store for him, he wouldn't have left Beirut even with a busted leg and nerves so shot to hell that his hands shook when he placed them on his typewriter keys. *You're lucky to be alive,* Rick had said. *When you get out of that hospital, come home.* So he'd come back to Canada, been taken fishing in the north country and told, in the nicest way possible, that he was all washed up. Oh, Rick had used other words. *Rest*, he'd said, *relaxation, take it easy for a while, no need to get back in the thick of things too quickly.* And he'd sweetened the pie with a bonus and a raise. But Geoff was no fool. When a war correspondent is taken off the political desk and dumped into sports, he'd have to be an idiot not to notice that he was demoted. And, when that sports beat didn't include something dignified like football, he'd have to be a total imbecile not to know he was being put out to pasture.

Thirty-six years old and plucked out of the action like some helpless child. The thought of it made Geoff's teeth grind together in an impotent fury. It wouldn't last, he'd made that vow to himself. His leg was healing, slowly it was true, but at least he could hobble around on it now. *The femur has been shot to smithereens*, the surgeon had said, *but we'll have you walking. We'll give you a romantic limp.* Romantic, hell. Pitiable was more like it. He'd been bedridden for weeks, in a cast for months. And, for a man who had taken his athletic prowess for granted, this new physical vulnerability had been damned hard to swallow. One step down the wrong street in Beirut, a bomb explosion, hours of lying under rubble next to a dead body. He'd gone half mad from the pain and had been convinced that he would suffocate to death. Those hours had changed his life. The Geoff Hamilton that he had known, the war correspondent with the front-page byline, the inimitable courage and the invincibility of a cat with nine lives, was gone. In his place was someone else; a man with memories, a helpless man, an angry one.

Well, he hadn't gone down without a fight. He'd argued like crazy, had said that his leg was on the mend, that his nerves were coming along nicely, but Rick had shaken his head.

'Don't rush it,' Rick had said.

They'd been sitting in front of the fire in the small cabin Rick had on Simpson Lake. It was a cosy place, with fishing and boating gear hanging on its logged walls, its interior warmed by an old-fashioned wood stove. Rick, a burly bear of a man, had built most of it himself and said that it was his idea of a retirement home. Geoff had always enjoyed his stays at the cabin, but this time he felt claustrophobic as if he couldn't breathe.

'Rush what? Going back to work? Look, Rick. I can get around . . .'

'With a cane.'

'All right,' he'd said impatiently. 'But I'll be off that soon.'

Rick had glanced at him with a sympathy that made Geoff's fists clench. 'You're not ready to go back to Beirut.'

'You don't have anyone else who can do the same job for you.'

'Brennan will go.'

'Brennan! He's too young, too inexperienced, too . . .'

'Geoff.' Rick put out a restraining hand to stop Geoff from standing up and pacing around. 'The doctor says you're not ready.'

They stared at one another, and Geoff had seen the implacability in the older man's eyes. They'd been friends for a decade of camaraderie that had included hard work, hard drinking and good times. Rick had hired him, but their relationship had been so friendly and casual that Geoff had almost forgotten who was the boss and who was the employee.

He'd swallowed his pride then and said desperately, 'I need to work. I can't go on like this.'

Rick gave him a comforting smile. 'I'm going to put you on the Petra Morgan swim.'

'The *what*?'

And that's how he found himself sitting at six o'clock on a fine June morning in a large metropolitan pool watching Petra Morgan swim. Geoff hadn't even known she existed until he'd come back to Canada.

He'd learned about her in one of the back issues of *McLean's* when he'd still been in his cast and forced into long periods of inactivity. Petra Morgan, the next Queen of the Lake, the schoolteacher turned swimmer who was going to conquer Lake Ontario. The reporter in *McLean's* had seemed enraptured with her, raving about her swimming skills, her training programme, her charm, her pretty smile. There'd been a picture with the article, a photograph of a dark-haired woman with wide cheekbones, a narrow chin, eyes of an indeterminate colour and a smile that put dimples into her cheeks. Geoff hadn't been interested enough in Petra Morgan or marathon swimming to do any more than skim the words and glance at the picture. He'd forgotten all about her the moment he'd put the magazine down. It wasn't until Rick had told him that he was going to cover Petra's swim in Lake Ontario that Geoff realised he'd read about her before.

And it wasn't until he actually met her that Geoff understood what sort of prejudices he'd had about women marathon swimmers. He had expected someone brawny, muscular, and chunky. In fact, when he'd first been introduced to her, he'd thought that someone was playing a joke on him. Instead of big shoulders, she had slender ones. Instead of muscular legs, hers were slim. The fact was that Petra Morgan was one of the most fragile-looking women he'd ever met. She was no more than five feet tall and, although she was in her midtwenties, she had a girl's figure; narrow in the hips, a slight bust, shoulder blades that looked like birds' wings. He couldn't believe that this was the woman who was supposed to swim across Lake Ontario. He knew he couldn't do it. He didn't think that she'd have a chance.

Not until he'd watched her training, that was. Then he'd had to grudgingly admit that beneath that fragility was a surprisingly steely strength and stamina. She seemed indefatigable, her body cutting through the water with efficiency and speed, her head turning to the side again and again, her legs doing a steady flutter kick, her arms going round and round. Geoff reluctantly gave her points for perseverance and felt a faint flicker of curiosity at what made her keep at it, hour after excruciating hour. Of course, that's what he was there to find out. That was his assignment. To cover Petra Morgan's crossing of Lake Ontario and to give newspaper readers some idea of what made her tick. The problem was that Geoff didn't really care. People were dying around the globe, men were being tortured by totalitarian governments, elections were being rigged and terrorists were threatening world peace. Who cared if one woman challenged a lake? Who cared how long it took her? Who gave a damn?

'She's great, isn't she?'

Geoff brought himself out of his reverie and turned to find Joe McGinnis beside him. The trainer was a small man with a barrel chest and hair cut shorter than a buck private's. He wore a whistle on a rope around his neck, a T-shirt that said 'Go, Petra, go,' and a pair of blue swimming trunks. His round face was wrinkled as if he spent most of his time outdoors, squinting against the sun.

'Yeah,' Geoff said.

Joe didn't notice his lack of enthusiasm, but then that was Joe. In the two days since he'd come to watch Petra swim, Geoff had realised that Joe's optimism and cheerfulness were unlimited. He grinned, he bounced, he waved his arms in the air, his conversation was a continual pep talk. And there was no quenching him. When it came to Petra Morgan, Joe was a bubbling fountain of facts, figures, and glowing endorsements. As far as Joe was concerned, Petra Morgan was a champion.

'And this is nothing,' Joe went on. 'Wait till you see her at the lake. This is child's play for her.'

'Yeah. I can see that.'

'I mean this was Petra's idea. I told her—go have a nice holiday before we go to the cottage—but she wanted to keep training. That's the way she is. Once Petra gets her mind on to something, she never quits.'

'Mmmmm.'

'And there's no stopping her. This young lady is going to break records, I can tell you that.'

Geoff nodded.

'Are you a swimmer?'

Geoff shrugged slightly. 'I know how to swim.'

Joe was now eyeing him in a professional sort of way, assessing the broad shoulders under Geoff's plaid short-sleeved shirt and the muscular curve of his arms. 'You look like you'd have the build of the sport.'

'I swam a lot as a kid, raced a bit. That was all.'

'You should think about doing it again. It would be a great sport for you now.'

'Now?'

'With your leg. That injury wouldn't stop you in the water. Not once you'd built up some stamina.'

Geoff looked down at the pool. He didn't like to talk about his leg with anyone. 'Yeah,' he said.

He missed the shrewdness of Joe's glance and the small smile. 'Of course, I'm not saying you'd want to be like Petra.'

Geoff was watching that slight figure with its unceasing motion. Up, around and over. 'No. I don't think I could stand it.'

Joe's eyes followed his. 'No,' he said reverently, standing up to head back to his place by the pool, 'most people couldn't. She's unique.'

Petra Morgan. The assignment would have been far more fascinating, Geoff thought as he once again shifted his leg and tried to ignore the pain that shot up it like an arrow into his groin, if Petra Morgan had been his type. But she wasn't. When he'd spoken to her, she'd answered him softly, looking at him quickly and then glancing away. She was shy, Geoff had judged, and he liked his women bold. And her looks didn't appeal to him. Not that she wasn't attractive. He supposed that she was pretty enough in a sort of ephemeral way. She had delicate bones in her face, short brown curly hair, wide grey eyes, a small nose and a mouth that was soft and rounded. But she lacked some of the physical characteristics that Geoff found particularly enticing in a woman. He went for leggy, curvaceous blondes with a bountiful pair of mammary glands. He didn't much care about their personalities, their intellect or their conversation. Being a war correspondent hadn't given Geoff much leisure time to develop a relationship with any of the women he'd bedded during his distinguished career.

Even as a boy, Geoff had known precisely what he wanted to be when he grew up. While his three other brothers took turns at wanting to be firemen, policemen, astronauts and jet pilots, Geoff had only one goal in mind. He wanted to be where the action was, where the decisions were being made, where the news was being created. He'd graduated with a degree in political science from the University of Toronto and started his journalistic career as a city reporter for the *Globe & Mail*. From there it was a short hop into national politics and then, after he'd been employed by a wire service, into the international arena. Geoff had the usual journalistic tricks up his sleeve. He knew how to ask the right questions and he had a flair with words, but it was his fearlessness that eventually put him in every hot spot around the globe. He'd been the last North-American journalist in Iran before the Khomeini take-over and the first in the Falklands. He'd been at the border of Afghanistan when the Russian tanks rolled in. And, when Beirut had flared into gunfire, Geoff had asked to go. That was the best part of being foot-loose and fancy free. Unlike many of his fellow journalists, he didn't have children waiting for him at home or a wife wondering if he'd ever come back alive.

Geoff had deliberately chosen to remain single. He refused to date a woman who seemed to have marriage on her mind and, if he noted a budding of any small domestic tendencies, he cut off the relationship swiftly and as painlessly as he could. He wasn't unkind; it was simply that he didn't have a lot of time or energy for slow disintegrations or tortuous partings. He was careful to let his wishes be known, and most women accepted him for what he was. And he'd never had any trouble finding partners. He was too good-looking, too charming, too rakish not to attract women in droves. His hair was blond and wavy, his eyes were blue as a sunlit sky, his nose straight, his chin square and determined. In his pragmatic way, Geoff accepted his looks as a gift and his attraction to women as a natural right. He didn't exploit his romantic accomplishments, nor did he blow them out of proportion. In his busy life, women came a long way after his job and their function was to provide him with a good time and a sexual release. Geoff believed in living hard and playing hard, and he did both with consummate ease.

'Time's up Petra.'

The swimming figure stopped its incessant motion and the capped head raised itself out of the water. 'Was that ten miles altogether, Joe?'

'Yup.'

Below Geoff, the training session was coming to an end. Petra was pulling herself out of the pool and was now standing at its edge, water running down the black sheen of her bathing suit and dripping on to the tile. She pulled off her goggles and then her bathing cap, shaking out her damp, dark curls. Geoff watched as she flexed her shoulder muscles and then talked earnestly to Joe. He couldn't quite catch her words, but he had a fair idea of what she'd be talking about. Timing, pacing, strokes per minute. Arrangements for the next training session. Receiving a Joe McGinnis pep talk. Geoff gave a silent and unsatisfying curse and wished himself anywhere except where he was, staring down at a slip of a woman who was obsessed with something as trivial as swimming across a lake. And he had no choice except to follow her around for the next month in order to send back a human interest story to Rick on her personality, her training, her courage and her life story. As if he cared. *Goddamn.*

'Eighty-five strokes per minute during that last sprint,' Joe said. 'You looked good.'

Petra nodded.

'And great form, sweetheart. If you can keep that up on the lake, you'll do just fine.'

Petra gave him a small smile and reached with one arm upwards and then the other to stretch out the muscles in her back. She was in top shape; she knew that, but her muscles would stiffen a bit. They always did.

'Petra, honey. We're going to break a record.'

'Joe, I don't know if breaking a record is as important as getting across. Thirty-two miles.' She sighed. 'I dream about it some nights.'

'You'll be ready for it. I give you my Joe McGinnis oath on that. By the time you make the swim, it'll be a piece of cake.'

Petra gave Joe a look of affection. He was President of the Lakeside Swimming Association, her own private coach and the father she'd never had. Ever since her childhood, Joe had bestowed upon her his attention and his enthusiasm, his caring and his concern. And, for him, she had swum hundreds of miles, trained for hours every day and stuck with her adolescent wish to swim Lake Ontario. It had been a wish that had been interrupted by the crisis with her mother, her education and her job, but she had never stopped swimming, even during the hardest times, and they'd both known that one day she would make the attempt.

When she'd told Joe that this summer was it, he had gone into high gear. He'd put her on a fitness

programme that included a two-hour daily swim; he'd
made the necessary arrangements with the Safety
Committee of the Ontario Solo Swim Association; and
he'd raised money and lined up the four boats and crew
that would accompany her across the lake. Petra had
had her medical certificate authorised and done the ten-
mile swim required in order to prove to the OSSA that
she was capable of crossing Lake Ontario. All that
remained now was another month of training before
they set the date.

'Until tomorrow then,' she said as she began to walk
off towards the showers.

'You have a breakfast meeting at 8.00 with that
newspaper chap.'

Petra stopped and glanced up towards the visitor's
benches where a blond head glistened under the lights.
'Oh,' she said.

Joe glanced at her downturned mouth. 'Now, Petra,
publicity is important or I wouldn't have agreed to
having him in the first place. When marathon
swimming is in the news, funding is a snap.'

'I know,' she said, turning on her heel, 'but that
doesn't mean I have to like it.'

Joe walked beside her, keeping up with her quick
pace. 'We're going to get a lot of coverage for this
swim, so you might as well get used to having him
around.'

It took a second, but then the realisation dawned on
Petra. 'You mean he's coming with us to the lake?'

Joe looked uncomfortable. 'That's right.'

'Joe,' she hissed, pulling open the door to the
women's shower room. 'You promised privacy, you
said I'd be on my own, you . . .'

'Now, Petra.' Joe glanced back at that figure in the
gallery and pushed Petra into the empty shower room,
letting the door close behind them. 'You don't want to
give him the idea that he isn't wanted.'

'Yes, I do,' she said heatedly.

'Bad publicity would be . . .'

'I don't want him probing around in my life. I don't want him asking questions. I'm a very private person, Joe. You know that.'

'You've got nothing to hide.'

Petra rolled her eyes to the ceiling. 'Only a father that skipped out when I was three and a mother who's a basket case. A charming family life that will look wonderful written up across the country.'

'That's not your story, sweetheart.'

'No, but that's how journalists think. Dig and probe. Scratch out the dirty parts. Look what happened to Caroline.'

Joe winced. Caroline was another one of his protégées, a racer who had gone on to win an Olympic medal. An enthusiastic press had followed her around for days after she'd returned to Canada and one eager beaver had discovered that Caroline was adopted, a fact that went out on the wire sevice to 200 newspapers. Caroline wasn't ashamed that she was adopted, but she was sensitive about it and so was her family. They'd cringed when they'd read about themselves in the press.

Petra saw the expression on Joe's face and softened. It wasn't his fault, she knew he was right. Renting the boats for a swim was expensive, training cost money and, although she had contributed her savings towards this swim, they'd needed extra money. A promise of publicity encouraged manufacturers to help back a swim, provided the swimmer wore one of their suits or a pair of their goggles or ate their health food. And private backers were not only delighted when their swimmer succeeded but also thrilled when the triumph was reported in the papers. It gave them the feeling that they'd been part of an historic moment.

'It's okay, Joe,' she said. 'I'll survive.'

It took a while for Joe's frown to unwrinkle. 'And you'll be pleasant to this fellow? You won't bite his head off?'

'I'll be on my best behaviour. Cross my heart and hope to die.'

Joe's grin was back. 'Good girl.' He glanced around him. 'Hey, I always did want to spend time in the ladies' shower. The trouble is . . .'

Petra filled in the pause for him. '. . . there's no ladies.'

Joe gave a dramatic sigh. 'The story of my life.' And then waving at her walked out.

Petra smiled to herself as she turned on a tap and stood under the hot, stinging water, letting its warmth flow down her. Joe, a former swimming champion himself, had a wife and twin daughters, now grown up and married. Neither of his girls had wanted to be anything more than casual swimmers, a fact that Joe had lamented long and loud to anyone who would listen. With that paternal gap in his life, he had been forced to take protégées under his wing, and many a medal-winner in Canada had once been a surrogate member of the McGinnis household. Joe and his wife, Sunny, nurtured his swimmers, coddled them, fed them and encouraged them. Petra was looking forward to her month's training, because she'd be staying at the McGinnis cottage on Indian Lake under Joe's tutelage and Sunny's motherly care. It was the closest she'd ever be to being part of a real family.

Petra sighed as she peeled off her bathing suit and hung it over the bar beside her towel. For the past few years, her mother had been an overriding concern. Sheila Morgan had had a nervous breakdown when Petra was in college and she'd never quite recovered from it. She still had trouble coping with life, not with the large problems that overwhelmed most people, but the smaller everyday concerns. Loud noises made her tremble, a day of events had her exhausted, the need to make a decision caused her to dither and ramble as if she were senile instead of fifty-five and in the best of health. Petra supposed that she could understand it.

Sheila had been under stress ever since her father had walked out of the house and never come back. She'd been forced to earn a living and care for a small, energetic child and, for a woman who was highly strung, nervous and prone to tears, it had been trying and difficult. She'd managed with minimal success for fifteen years, finally falling to pieces when she'd had that accident. It had been a small thing, a slide on an icy pavement, a cracked ankle and a twisted wrist. But, Petra supposed, it was the final straw in a life that had been one long accumulation of accidents and failures.

Now, Sheila spent half her time in a mental institution and half her time in her flat. With each release, Petra prayed that her mother would finally have returned to normal, but within a few months the same story was repeated over and over again. The teary phone calls would begin, the tales of strangers following her down the streets would start anew, food would be prepared and not eaten, and drugs would be taken to the point of overdose. It was a pattern of behaviour that had begun when Petra was a child and had only grown worse with time.

Even when she was very small, Petra had understood that there was something not quite right with Sheila, something that set her apart from the other mothers she knew. By the time she was eight, she had learned not to ask her mother for the sort of things most children wanted. Sheila couldn't have taken the stress of being class mother or baking cakes for Brownies or throwing a birthday party for exuberant children. And, by the time she was in high school, Petra was in charge of the flat, the shopping and the meals. With each passing year, Petra had taken over more and more of her mother's tasks until it had reached the point where the role reversal was complete. When she was sixteen, Petra had awoken one night to hear her mother whimpering in her bed. 'A bad dream,' she had said, crying. 'Such a terrible bad dream.' And Petra had put her arms around Sheila, comforted her until she went back to sleep again, and understood with a terrible sort of finality that she no longer had, in any true sense of the word, a mother.

Swimming had been her salvation. There had been a municipal pool close to her home, and she'd gone there all during the summers and every weekend in the winters. One of the lifeguards had noticed her and suggested that she take some classes. By the time she was fourteen, Petra had done the full round of Red Cross lessons, having already earned her bronze medallion in lifesaving. She took her National Lifeguard at sixteen and her Water Safety Instructor's course at seventeen. She'd had absolutely no urge to race so it wasn't until she heard Joe speak at a meeting for instructors that it occurred to her that perhaps she was a marathon swimmer. She'd gone up to him during the coffee break and waited until he was alone.

'Yes?'

'My name's Petra Morgan, and I'm interested in long-distance swimming.'

'Are you?' Joe had eyed her as if she were specimen under a microscope.

'Yes.'

'I don't take on anyone who's half-hearted.'

'I understand that.'

'And,' he'd growled, 'if you've got a romance going in your life, you might as well kiss it goodbye.'

She'd given him a shy smile. 'There's no one.'

'And it'll hurt. Really hurt.'

'I can handle it.'

'Hmmmph.' Joe had appraised her at length and then said, grudgingly, 'Show up at the Lakeside Pool at six o'clock tomorrow morning. I'll try you out then.'

The try-out had been painful, utterly exhausting and one of the most exhilarating things she'd ever done. To this day, Petra didn't know exactly how many miles she swam that morning as Joe put her through the paces, doing the sprints, giving her ten-second intervals to catch her breath and then starting her on them all over again. All she knew was that she loved it; loved pushing her body to its limits, loved knowing that she'd conquered the distance, loved the sensation of euphoria she had while swimming. When it was over and she'd pulled herself out of the pool on shaking arms, he'd said gruffly, 'Well, think you can do it?'

Petra had lifted her chin. 'Yes.'

He narrowed his eyes and gave her a severe look which Petra later came to realise accompanied a softening of the heart. 'Think you can put up with me at five o'clock in the morning, Monday to Friday?'

'Yes.'

'And, what precisely do you want to swim?'

The answer to that question was easy. Petra could see it in her mind's eye: an enormous expanse of water, blue and sparkling under the sun, its waves capped in little white peaks. 'The lake,' she'd said.

He'd known, of course, which lake she was referring to. 'Is that right?' he'd asked.

'Yes.'

'Hummph.' A further narrowing of the eyes. 'And when precisely would you want to do it?'

'Next year,' she'd said.

'Next year,' he'd echoed. 'Next year. Well, we'll see.'

But the following year had brought so much disruption and financial difficulties into Petra's life that she'd been forced to cancel her plans. Sheila's mental state had finally disintegrated to the point that she had to stop work and go into an institution, leaving Petra with only the small amount of savings they'd accumulated over the years. The only way that Petra could attend university was to combine her scholarship with a thirty-hour-a-week job waitressing. Training for the lake swim had been impossible, but by then she'd become a treasured member of the McGinnis entourage, and Joe had waved off her apologies and said to just keep up with the work-outs. After graduating from college, she'd found a position teaching grade-three children and a summer job as a waterfront counsellor with a camp. It had taken Petra five years before she felt financially solvent enough to leave her summer job and start training again.

She'd spent the winter months with a relatively easy work-out programme that progressed to greater difficulty as the spring months rolled around. She was now up to ten to fifteen-mile swims in the pool. When she went to the McGinnis cottage on Indian Lake, Joe would push her up to twenty. Petra winced a bit as she contemplated it and then turned off the shower, reaching for the towel she'd hung over a bar. Twenty miles, she thought, rubbing her wet hair. Days and days of swimming, evenings of pleasant conversation, eating Sunny's good food and ... Petra remembered the reporter and, making a grimace, rubbed her head furiously. She didn't want him at the cottage, poking around, asking questions, trying to delve into her psyche. She knew what he was going to want. A human interest story. *What Makes Petra Swim So Hard?* And she'd seen from his face that he wasn't going to be got rid of easily.

Her only conversation with Geoffrey Hamilton so far had been brief, casual and not at all friendly. She'd met him the morning before when she arrived at the pool at 5:00 a.m. for her usual work-out. Joe had made the introductions.

'Petra, honey, this is Geoff Hamilton. He's working for Allied Press, and he wants to do a story on you.'

'Hello, Miss Morgan.' He'd had to lean on his cane to stretch out his hand.

'Hello,' she'd said, letting her small hand slip into his large one.

'You don't mind if I watch you swim a bit, do you?'

She'd glanced up at him then. Although his voice held an amiable tone, his face was unsmiling, his mouth grim as if he were angry. But the severity of his expression didn't harm his good looks at all. Petra didn't think she'd ever seen any man so handsome. Blond hair the colour of wheat at sunset, deep-set blue eyes under golden brows, an aquiline nose, and a mouth that could have been carved in porcelain so firm was it . . . so . . . She'd looked away from him and back down to their clasped hands.

'No,' she said, 'I don't mind.'

But she hadn't known then that Geoff Hamilton was going to follow her around for the next month, trying to pin her down, trying to dissect her like a butterfly held to a board with its wings tacked down and spread wide so that every marking could be examined, touched, revealed. Petra wrapped the towel around her body, crumpled her wet bathing suit into a ball, her hands clenched tightly around it, and walked into the dressing room. She was a private person, just as she had told Joe. Private to the point that she was incapable of expressing emotion, of describing her inner feelings, of explaining herself. She'd always been that way. Even as a child she'd been quiet and restrained. Her teachers had found her easy to handle; she'd practically faded into the woodwork in high school. She hadn't wanted anyone to notice her, she hadn't wanted any friends. Petra had been well aware of the protocol of having friends. You were supposed to invite them to your house for lunch and for overnights. When you were a teenager, boys came to talk to your parents before they took you out on a date. But Petra had been ashamed and terrified of bringing anyone home, male or female. The flat was small, cluttered and, although she tried to keep it clean, often dirty. And Sheila was totally unpredictable. She could be congenial one moment or crazy the next. Petra had cringed at the thought of having any of her acquaintances meet her mother.

The habits of childhood and adolescence had stayed with her. She knew she didn't mix well with people; she often felt awkward, stiff and uncomfortable. And she was worse with men, not men like Joe who treated her like a daughter, but men who looked at her with a sexual interest. They gave her the feeling that she was being pursued and, like any wild animal who was afraid of restraint, she fled from them. It wasn't as if Petra hadn't tried to have a normal relationship; she had and it had bombed unmercifully. She'd had a brief affair with another teacher that she had met at a friend's party. She had done what was asked of a modern woman in the hopes that proving herself at the rituals of a sexual encounter would mean that she was as psychologically sound as anyone else. She had gone out with him on one date and gone to bed with him on the second. There had been a flurry of activity over a month's time that had camouflaged his smugness at having possessed her and her growing panic at the discovery that, not only didn't she like him very much, she absolutely abhorred sex with him. It was a groping, loveless thing that left her feeling unsatisfied and close to tears. He, on the other hand, always wanted to do it again.

Petra had been too confused to know where to place the blame; she only knew that she had to cut the relationship off before she died of suffocation from his embrace, his closeness, his wanting of her. And, when it was finally over with relief on her side and recrimination on his, Petra had vowed to herself that she'd never get involved like that again. Life seemed far safer to her when she was by herself, free from anyone's wants and desires and accountable to no one. She accepted herself as different from other women and ignored any feelings of loneliness. She swam instead. Laps and more laps. Miles upon miles, her mind slipping into that other space, that other dimension where nothing hurtful or painful existed. She had never been able to describe that space to anyone. It defied measurement or analysis; it defied explanation.

Which was why Petra hated the thought of Geoffrey Hamilton probing away at her, digging through her protective layers, trying to find the core of her. And he didn't look like the type who would be easily fobbed off with superficial answers and facile explanations. He'd want depth, reasons, meanings, and he had a whole month in which to scrape away at her for them. Petra, who had looked forward to that month with Joe and Sunny, found herself no longer wanting to go. Not even all the McGinnis' love and affection would be able to make up for Geoffrey Hamilton's presence. His being there would poison the atmosphere and pollute her one little corner of the world.

Petra threw her bathing suit down on a bench, a small angry sound rising out of her lips. She'd be pleasant to him, all right, She wouldn't bite his head off, as she had promised, but she'd be damned if she'd do anything else for him. She would answer questions only when they were asked and talk only when spoken to. The rest of the time she would swim, swim and swim some more. She was going to make certain that Geoffrey Hamilton's stay at Indian Lake was one of the most wasted months of his life. And, if he wanted to keep up to her, he was going to have to swim. Lap after lap. Mile after mile. The thought of it made her smile a bit. There were very few men in this world who could match Petra Morgan when she was in the water and, as far as she knew, Geoffrey Hamilton wasn't one of them.

CHAPTER TWO

PETRA and Geoff had breakfast in a small coffeeshop in a shopping centre near the pool. Petra had changed into a pair of jeans and a white T-shirt that said, 'I'm going, Joe', in bright red letters. Both her T-shirt and Joe's had been gifts from Sunny who claimed that now they wouldn't have to converse any more, they could let their shirts do the talking. She wore no make-up, and her hair was still damp from her swim and curled in a dark chaos around her head, tendrils sticking to her forehead and temples. On her feet were a scuffed pair of leather sandals with thongs, the kind that encircle the big toe and hang on from there. It was a typical Petra ensemble, and she was well aware that it did nothing to add to her femininity. Instead the snug fit of the jeans and loose T-shirt only served to emphasise the boyish shape of her figure. She liked outfits like that. They didn't advertise anything that she wasn't prepared to offer.

'That was quite a swim you did this morning,' Geoff said. He'd ordered cottage cheese and fruit and was watching Petra dig into eggs, bacon and toast.

'It's a standard work-out,' she replied. 'Ten miles, five of them in sprints.'

'Is that how you've been training all spring?'

She shook her head. 'Joe's been increasing the distance every month.'

'Tell me about Joe.'

Petra looked up at him in surprise. 'Joe? Aren't you going to interview him yourself?'

'I'd like another perspective.'

She shrugged, bit into her toast and said, 'Well, he's dedicated and a great coach. I've known him for years.'

'How many?'

'About eight.'

'What made you decide to use him?'

'I didn't know anyone else coaching marathon swims.'

'And . . .'

'And . . .? Well, nothing. We got together and now he coaches me.' Petra sprinkled some salt and pepper on her scrambled eggs.

'He thinks you're wonderful.'

She didn't smile at that, but merely ate some eggs. 'He should think that,' she finally said.

Geoff gave her an amused look. 'Isn't that a bit egotistical?'

Her eyes, grey between their fringe of dark lashes, appraised him. 'No,' she said. 'He worked hard to get me to the point where he could believe that.'

'Do you have to believe that, too? So that you can get across the lake?'

That was precisely the sort of question that Petra didn't like. It was the thin end of the wedge, trying to push between the cracks in her protective layer. 'I trust Joe's opinion,' she said.

'Tell me, Petra, why do you do it?'

'Do what?' she asked, reaching for a jar of marmalade on the lazy susan in the middle of the table. But her hand was caught in mid-air and held between fingers that gripped like a vice.

'Swim,' Geoff said grimly.

Petra stared at their hands. His fingers were long, his palm was warm and hard, the back of his hand was dusted with golden hairs. He had a silver digital watch on his wrist and his forearm, also coated with gold hair, was muscular and tensed. He was a big man, close to six feet tall, and she could feel the power of him in his hand, trapping her fingers but holding them in such a way that he didn't crush the delicate bones.

'Is this an interviewing technique?' she asked coldly, and he let go of her hand.

'You didn't answer my question,' he said.

'I swim because I want to.'

His eyes narrowed. 'That's meaningless.'

Petra had pulled her hand down beneath the table and, unconsciously, she rubbed it. 'Not to me.'

'Well, it's not good enough.'

'It's the best I can do.'

Geoff leaned forward, impaled her on that blue glance. 'Why don't you want to co-operate with me?'

'I'm co-operating.'

'The hell you are,' he grated. 'You haven't given me one straight answer.'

'Look,' she said angrily, her promise to Joe completely forgotten, 'I'm a swimmer and that's all. I want to go up to that lake and swim. I plan to sleep, eat and breathe swimming. I don't want to spend my precious time talking about things that don't matter.'

'What are you afraid of?'

She sat back. 'Afraid? I'm not afraid of anything.'

'Secrets? Black sheep in the family? Skeletons in the cupboard?'

Petra took a deep breath. 'I don't like reporters.'

Geoff gave her a grin. Even Petra had to admit to herself that it was a very attractive grin. It turned up the corners of his mouth and wrinkled the skin around his eyes. It gave him a boyish air that was very appealing.

'Look,' he said, 'I took a shower this morning. I brushed my teeth. I keep my nails clean. A lot of people think I'm a perfectly nice fellow.'

'It's not *you*. It's what you *are*.'

'Ah, a generic journalist-hater. Have I got that right?'

'Yes,' she said defiantly. She wouldn't let him make fun of her.

Geoff sighed and poked at his cottage cheese. 'All right. Let's face the facts. I've been asked to do a feature on marathon swimming in general and you in particular. Joe McGinnis invited me up to his cottage and on the swim so I could do a decent job. He's thrilled to have me there, because he thinks my articles will push the cause of long-distance swimming. You, on the other hand, would like me to drop dead today and leave you alone. Right?'

'Right.'

'But I can't. So what's next?'

'That's your problem.'

'You're all heart, Miss Morgan, aren't you?'

She ignored him. 'Why don't you go back to your editor and ask for a change of assignment? You must do other things, don't you? Like cover politics or something?'

'Believe me,' Geoff said coldly, 'I'd rather be anywhere than sitting in this restaurant and trying to convince you that I'm a nice guy.'

'So why not leave?'

Geoff leaned forward and jabbed a finger in her direction. 'You know something? I can't help thinking that there's some little thing you're trying to hide.'

Petra gave a small shrug. 'There's nothing. I told you that.'

But Geoff wasn't the kind to give up when he was on the scent of something. 'A sad childhood, perhaps? An unhappy love affair?' He looked at her bent head. 'Yeah, that must be it. Got jilted, did you?'

Petra's head came up quickly, her eyes wide and startled.

Geoff, knowing that he had hit pay-dirt, went on. 'Everyone has something to hide, Miss Morgan. I've been a journalist long enough to recognise that fact. And it's often something like an affair gone sour. You'd be surprised how many people will try to . . .'

But Petra wasn't going to let him continue. He had come far too close to her already, and she needed to deflect him, to turn him in some other direction. She gave him a smile, knowing that there was no defence like a good attack. 'I can't figure out why they put you

on this assignment,' she said. 'I'll bet you don't know
the first thing about marathon swimming.'

Geoff stiffened slightly. 'I'll learn on the job. That's
why I've been given a month to do it.'

'That's irresponsible, isn't it?'

'What?'

'Your editor giving you this assignment. He should
have got someone with experience, a former swimmer
perhaps, a . . .'

Geoff's lips tightened. 'It's none of your damned
business as far as I can see.'

But Petra had sensed his vulnerability. 'And I think
you hate the idea of following me around anyway. So
why not go back to your boss and tell him you want
out.' She nibbled on a piece of bacon. 'We'd both be
happier that way.'

Geoff stood up, his cottage cheese and fruit uneaten.
'We might both be happier,' he said through clenched
teeth, 'but I'm just like you, Miss Morgan. Stubborn as
hell.' And with that, he was gone.

Petra watched him limp out of the restaurant and
then sighed, her anger seeping out of her and leaving
her feeling empty and unhappy with herself. She had
done exactly the opposite of what she had intended to
do, which was treat Geoffrey Hamilton with a distant
courtesy and careless nonchalance. And she'd broken
her promise to Joe which wasn't right because Joe was
so faithful in keeping *his* promises to her. And she
understood Joe's rationale, which was that having one
reporter on the site was far better than being hassled by
half a dozen when she was ready to make the swim. By
promising Allied Press exclusive coverage, Joe was
making sure that her attempt to cross the lake wouldn't
turn into a media circus.

But something about Geoffrey Hamilton brought out
the worst in Petra. It couldn't be the way he looked
because he had an exceedingly pleasing appearance.
Not even his limp could hide the fact that he was a well-

made man, muscular and even graceful at times. And he
had a classically handsome face, the kind that women
fell for in droves, and Petra wasn't any more immune to
good looks than anyone else. No, it was something else.
She'd felt an anger in him, an antagonism that belied
whatever charm he had intended to exert on her. Even
at the beginning of their conversation, Petra had sensed
that Geoffrey Hamilton didn't like her and that he had
taken this assignment unwillingly and without enthusiasm. She didn't know why that was so; after all, they
were strangers to one another. But she wasn't the type
to become a shrinking violet in the face of someone
else's dislike. She had reacted quite naturally to him,
even considering that, being a journalist, he had one
strike against him already. And, Petra saw no reason to
change the way she felt about him despite the fact that
she really didn't know the first thing about Geoffrey
Hamilton except that he was a good-looking man with
a limp, a disarming smile and an uncanny way of
finding her emotional scars. But that was more than
sufficient. Petra didn't like Geoffrey Hamilton at all.

Despite Geoff's innate stubbornness and his words to
Petra, he found himself later that afternoon, striding
(well, limping angrily really) into the offices of Allied
Press. It was a busy place with typewriters clacking
away, phones ringing constantly and people running
from one desk to another. Like any media centre, it ran
on hype, adrenalin and nerves. Geoff had always liked
visiting the office for short periods of time; usually he
thrived on the atmosphere, the agitation and the feeling
that he was close to the centre of things. But, on this
afternoon, he couldn't have cared less. He pushed his
way past the front desk, nodding abruptly to the
secretary and receptionist and then wove his way past
the other reporters until a hand was placed on his arm.

'Geoff,' a soft voice said.

He turned to find a pretty blonde smiling at him. She

was his type; tall, blonde, curvaceous and endowed with a pair of legs that went on endlessly. Geoff gave an inward groan and an outward grin. 'Marnie,' he said.

'It's been a long time.'

'Two years?'

'Yes.'

Geoff took a deep breath and leaned against a desk. 'So—how are you doing?'

She chattered on a bit while Geoff wondered what was the proper protocol in dealing with an ex-lover. He had made the mistake two years ago of mixing business with pleasure and going out with Marnie when he'd been in Toronto on a month's vacation. He usually had a policy of not dating women who worked at Allied Press, but no one else had been available at the time and Geoff had an acknowledged weakness for pretty, long-legged blondes. Marnie had been willing, eager and non-possessive, at least that's what she'd said, but he could tell by the look in her blue eyes that, now he was back, she was counting on seeing him again.

'. . . and you? I hear you've been put on the sports beat.'

Geoff lifted his cane slightly. 'I got some war wounds.'

'Yes, we heard all about it.' She paused. 'Are you living in Toronto now?'

Geoff went into a long and detailed explanation of his flat-hunting while he pondered the possibility of dating Marnie again. He had nothing against her; she was pleasant, smiled a lot and was easy on the eyes, but that's as far as it went. She was neither intellectually stimulating nor, when he got right down to it, was she physically exciting. Despite the curves and long legs, she'd been ho-hum in the sack. And Geoff could imagine what would happen if he did make a pass again. This time Marnie would take it more seriously. She might misconstrue such an action as meaning more than it did. She might think, God forbid, that his interest in her had something to do with romance, with love, with commitment ... or even worse, with marriage.

'. . . so right now I'm camping out in a hotel,' he said.

'Oh.'

Her smile had definitely acquired that come-hither quality. Geoff shifted uneasily. 'Well, if you'll excuse me, I've got to see Rick.'

'Stop by my desk on your way out and we can go for coffee.'

'Yeah ... well, I'll have to see how it goes.'

'Sure,' she said. 'I'm easy.'

That was the trouble, Geoff decided, as he limped off to Rick's office. Marnie was too easy. He could tell, just from the wishful look in her blue eyes, just how very easy she was going to be. A niggling dissatisfaction that had been growing in him began to flower into a positive irritation. Without quite realising it, Geoff had got tired of easy women. He could charm them, seduce them, slip into their willing bodies with almost no effort at all. Like ten pins, they fell before him in numbers so large he'd lost count of them. When he looked back upon his amorous past, Geoff could only remember the names of two women he'd slept with; his first, a girl in high school, and his last, a French journalist in Beirut. That thought brought him up sharp. It suddenly occurred to him that he hadn't had sex since his accident, that he'd been celibate for ... what was it? Three months? Ninety days. He calculated quickly—two thousand, one hundred and sixty hours. God, no wonder his frustration level was so low. And Rick, damn his hide, wanted to send him into nowhere's land to watch Petra Morgan swim.

'Geoff! Welcome to the inner sanctum.' Rick hurried around his desk and picked up the mass of papers that lay on his office's only other chair. 'I thought you'd be packing.'

Geoff carefully negotiated himself into a seated

position, hanging his cane on the back of the chair. Even so, the pain shot up his leg and he grimaced, unable to hide his expression from Rick.

'The leg still bothers you that much?'

Geoff took a deep breath. 'Less than it did. More than I like.'

'A month's rest in the sun won't harm you a bit.'

Geoff shifted in his seat. 'That's what I came to talk about.'

'What?'

'The Morgan swim. I want off the assignment.'

Rick ran his fingers through his thinning dark hair and sighed. 'Why?'

'Have you met her? Petra Morgan?'

'Uh-uh.'

'Consider yourself lucky then.'

'You didn't get along with her?'

'That's putting it mildly. She's argumentative, prickly, irritating, uncooperative and . . .'

Rick was grinning. 'No kidding.'

Geoff leaned forward. 'I'm not joking, Rick. I can't stand her.'

Rick leaned back in his swivelling chair. 'I didn't think you would.'

Geoff sat up. 'You didn't?'

'Hell, no. You didn't want to cover the swim in the first place. But I thought your antagonism might give the story a nice edge.'

'She doesn't like me either.'

Rick gave him a look of mock-shock. 'Hey, where's the Hamilton charm? Since when can a woman resist you?'

Geoff's smile was sour. 'Take me off the story, Rick.'

'And do what? You want to work in here?'

'Here?'

'The office. Editing stories, that sort of thing. You're not ready to go out in the field yet, Geoff.' He paused. 'But frankly, I can't see you in here either. You hate being cooped up.'

Geoff thought of Marnie, sitting at her desk and waiting to pounce on him when he left Rick's office. He imagined all the uncomfortable and embarrassing situations that could arise if he worked near her. He envisaged weeks of trying to avoid her eager conversation, her suggestive smiles, her pleading eyes.

'You're right,' he said. 'I'd hate it.'

'The Morgan swim is perfect for you right now. You'll have nothing to do but talk, watch her train and get a good tan.'

'Give me a city hall beat. That's not strenuous.'

'I can't take it away from Fuller.'

'Opera,' Geoff said desperately. 'That doesn't require a lot of energy.'

'Know the difference between a contralto and a mezzo-soprano?'

'Heart operations, then.'

'Give up, Geoff. It's Morgan or the office.'

Geoff's expletive described the sexual act in one brief and concise word.

'Besides,' Rick said, putting his fingers together to form a tent and contemplating the ceiling, 'I get the distinct impression that there's more to you and Morgan than meets the eye.'

'What do you mean?'

'Maybe all that antagonism is hiding something.'

'Like what?'

'Like an attraction, maybe?'

Geoff shot up out of his seat, cursed at the pain in his leg and grabbed his cane. Leaning against the chair, he pointed it directly at Rick as if it were a gun and said, 'I never heard anything so crazy in my life.'

'Yeah?'

'Yeah. You must be going soft in the head.'

Rick lifted both hands in an attitude of surrender. 'All right,' he said with a grin, 'but just don't shoot.'

Geoff lowered his cane and limped out of the office, but Rick could hear him muttering all the way down the hall. 'Attraction, my eye.'

Petra drove her Toyota over the rocks, the gravel and
the ridges with the sort of competence that comes from
experience. She was used to the road that led to Indian
Lake. It was unmetalled, only one car wide and curved
like a race track. If she went too slowly on it, the car
would be enveloped in its own dust and she'd be jolted
with every bump and crevice. If she drove too fast,
she'd lose control over the car and end up in a ditch
filled with brackish water, pussy willows and God
knows what kind of animal life. The secret was to go at
just the right speed so that the tyres of the car skimmed
over the bumps and the acceleration allowed her to
control a steering-wheel that tried to fight loose from
her hands.

What she had to ignore, and did with only minor
success, was that the jolting and banging was doing
awful things to the Toyota itself. It creaked and
groaned, squeaked and whined, and Petra winced at the
sounds. The car was on its last legs, but she didn't have
even the beginnings of a down-payment for a new one.
As the trees flashed by and the sun glinted down
between their leaves to make flickering patterns on her
windscreen, she tried to mentally calculate what her
financial position would be after the swim. There was
the flat rent, she thought, food, insurance, clothes for
autumn, Sheila's expenses if she were out of hospital
(thank heavens for the Ontario Health Plan that
covered her hospitalisation and drugs), the balance
owed on her Visa credit card, her membership at a
YWCA, her ... Petra bounced as the car hit an
unusually big bump and guessed with a sense of despair
that she'd be in a negative financial situation if the
Toyota died on her. Very negative.

She shook herself slightly and put thoughts of car
and money out of her head. She was very adept at
doing that sort of mental trick, and it stood her in good

stead when she was swimming. She didn't let unpleasant
thoughts plague her; she had learned to control her
mind patterns, to concentrate on what was important,
to even, if need be, let her brain go into neutral, an
ability that was invaluable when she was swimming mile
after repetitious mile and the pain would strike in her
shoulders or her legs. Ignoring muscular distress was
the only way she could continue to swim and, after a
while, she would find that she had worked through the
pain and that it had gone as quickly as it had come.

So now, when thoughts of the Toyota troubled her,
Petra switched into another mental gear. She cheerfully
contemplated the road ahead and the warm welcome
she'd get from Joe and Sunny. She conjured up images
of the cottage and enjoyed thinking about how simple
her life was going to be for a month. There were no
telephone wires into the lake to bring in the intrusion of
the outside world, no newspapers delivered with tales of
tragedy and disaster, no social events that required
dressing up or the application of cosmetics. And she let
pleasant memories of the warm blue waters of Indian
Lake, the shadows of overhanging trees, and the sounds
of birds and squirrels drift through her head. She did
not think about Geoffrey Hamilton at all. She had quite
firmly put him out of her mind after that breakfast. She
had no real hope that he'd give up the assignment and
knew that she'd have to put up with his presence at the
cottage. But she didn't bother to speculate about him,
ponder about him or venture any hypotheses about
what he would do or what he would say. She mentally
ignored any thought of him, and that was very
satisfactory.

The road, a narrow canyon between tightly gathered
trees, ended with an abruptness that was always
startling, opening out into a cleared area that held the
cottage, a small boathouse and a shed where Joe kept
all his tools and equipment. Like many cottages in
northern Ontario, the McGinnis abode had the

rambling look that comes with additions and annexes. Joe and Sunny had bought the cottage many years before when it was a one-room cabin and had added on to it in bits and pieces. It now had four bedrooms, a porch that wrapped around the front and one side and a summer kitchen that overlooked the lake. It wasn't luxurious but it was comfortable, furnished with sturdy beds and tables, rocking-chairs and cushioned seats under every window.

The sound of Petra's car in the driveway brought Sunny out of the side door along with Rembrandt, her large black Labrador and Renoir, a silver and black tabby cat of no particular origin. Petra climbed out of the car and was practically assaulted by the animals. Rembrandt liked to greet arrivals with a lick on the face, while Renoir cultivated an intense curiosity about the insides of automobiles. Petra almost tripped over her as she scooted underneath the car door and leaped on to the back of the front seat.

'Down, Remmie, you crazy fool of a dog.' Sunny grabbed the Labrador by his collar and pulled him off Petra.

'I'd be more flattered,' Petra said with a laugh, 'if I didn't know how undiscriminating Remmie is.'

The other woman gave her a resounding kiss on the cheek and a huge hug, enveloping Petra's slight figure in her larger one. Sunny was a big woman, several inches taller than Joe, big-boned and big-hearted. She had bright blue eyes, a freckled complexion and a mouth that seemed to have been made for smiling. Her hair, which had once been a bright red, was now sandy and streaked with grey. She wore it piled on top of her head in an untidy chignon. And, as usual, she was dressed in a T-shirt, overalls and sneakers.

They hugged for a moment and then, with an exclamation of surprise, Sunny pushed Petra away and held her at arm's length. 'Bones!' she said. 'My God, you're all bones. What have you been doing, starving yourself to death? And you're pale, too. Heavens, but you look terrible.'

Petra grinned. A lot of people might have been offended by the way Sunny assumed that she could pass judgment, but Petra wasn't one of them. She loved having Sunny fuss over her, scold her and take care of her. It was the sort of mothering that Shiela had been incapable of providing, and Petra had spent her childhood starving for any tiny morsel of affection that happened to be thrown her way. Even now that she was grown up, the hunger had remained, a seemingly insatiable desire to be pampered. Not that she let many people close enough to sense that need in her. Sunny was one of the very few that Petra allowed to slip past the high wall of defence she had erected around herself.

'Sunny, you're always full of compliments.'

But Sunny didn't seem to be listening. 'Potatoes,' she was murmuring, 'and lots of buttered biscuits. Vegetables, too. Spinach has iron; you look like you need that. Vitamins, calcium, and protein. You're going to have some colour in your cheeks and fat on your bones before *I* let you swim Lake Ontario.'

'Aye, aye, sir,' Petra said meekly.

'Did you travel light or heavy?'

'Light.' Petra opened up the back door of the car, shooed Renoir off the seat where she was perched and indicated her suitcase. 'Bathing suits and sweats.'

'I am,' Sunny said, 'putting you in the Emerald Room.'

Sunny had once, in a fit of mock-grandeur, given pretentious names to all the tiny, cramped bedrooms in the cottage. The Emerald Room was a cubby-hole off the main porch with a bed that had a green spread.

'I thought that one was for visiting royalty,' Petra said.

'Nope. The Queen now gets the Blue Room.'

'The Blue Room?'

'The back one with the turquoise garbage pail.'

'Real luxury,' Petra said.

'That's what she said in her thank-you note.'

Petra gave Sunny a quizzical look. 'The Queen?'

'Of course, who else?'

'Right,' Petra said, pulling out her suitcase. 'You know, Sunny, you're still as batty as you used to be.'

'Hah!' said Sunny. '*You're* always full of compliments.'

Petra was still smiling when she reached the porch, and she almost failed to notice the figure sitting on a wicker chair in one corner. She stopped short when she saw him, sought for some properly polite remark and ended up saying the first thing that came into her mind. 'So you're here.'

Geoff leaned back in his chair and gave her a long glance, his eyes taking in her tousled hair, T-shirt, torn jean shorts, dusty bare legs and sandalled feet. 'I said I would be, didn't I?'

Sunny, bewildered by this exchange, stepped in brightly. 'You've met, of course,' she said, 'so I don't have to bother with useless introductions. Geoff arrived yesterday, Petra, and made us biscuits last night. Very good they were, too.'

Geoff was dressed more casually than he'd been for that breakfast. He was wearing a blue tank top and navy shorts, an outfit that revealed a body that was hard and muscular. His bad leg was propped up on a stool and Petra briefly glanced at the scar that ran down the inside of his thigh, its whiteness cutting through the golden hairs. For a second, she wondered where he had got it and then inwardly shrugged, thinking, why should I care?

'Yes,' she said coldly, answering Geoff's question, 'you did.' Then she tugged her suitcase higher, threw open the screen door and walked into the cottage.

Sunny threw a puzzled look at Geoff who merely gave her a nonchalant shrug, and followed Petra inside.

When they reached the small bedroom, she watched as Petra put her suitcase on the bed and then said, 'What was that all about?'

'What?'

'That interchange on the porch.'

'Oh, that.' Petra opened the suitcase.

Sunny sat down on the bed and firmly closed the suitcase again. 'No unpacking until you give me some idea what's wrong.'

Petra sighed and rubbed her hair. 'He's a reporter.'

'So?'

'And I've met him and we don't get on.'

'He seems quite pleasant to me,' Sunny said. 'He arrived yesterday, and he has already endeared himself to my heart.'

'You've always been a sucker for a man who makes biscuits.'

'And I say a man who likes to cook can't be all bad.'

Petra flopped down on the bed and pulled off her sandals. 'I came here to swim, Sunny, not to be pestered by the press.'

'Hmmm. Joe thinks the coverage is a good thing.'

'Joe isn't going to be under scrutiny the way I am.'

'Now, Petra, don't go all huffy and prickly. A few questions never hurt anyone, and you've nothing to hide.'

'I just don't like . . .'

Sunny put her hand on Petra's arm. 'I know how you feel, dear, but he seems to be a nice enough fellow and God knows he's easy on the eyes. Now, we all have to be here together for a month. A little civility would help.'

Petra immediately felt guilty for being a rotten guest. No matter how much the McGinnises made it seem otherwise, she was no more a part of their family than Geoff was. And she had no right to abuse their hospitality and ruin their month at the cottage. 'I'm sorry,' she said. 'Of course, I'll be nice to him. It's just

that . . .' she gave Sunny a shy smile, 'I had wanted it to
be just us. You know, relaxed and easy. No
complications.'

Sunny gave her a hug. 'Of course you did and so did
I. But you know how Joe is. He loves to invite people to
the cottage, and he's miserable if he isn't training half a
dozen swimmers at once. Take Jennifer, for instance.
He dropped her into my lap last minute.'

'Jennifer?'

'The next great Canadian hope for the freestyle.'

Petra struggled with that for a moment, trying to
remember past conversations with Joe and mentions of
a teenager that he was grooming for the Olympics. 'I
thought Joe was training a boy for that.'

'Oh, good heavens, no,' Sunny said, shaking her head
with a sigh. 'Not Jennifer. There's nothing boyish about
that child in the least. She's one hundred and fifty
percent female. Wait until you see her.'

Petra had her chance to get a taste of what the month
was going to be like that night at dinner, and she
considered herself lucky that she didn't walk away from
the table in a state of complete indigestion.

Joe, of course, was pleased as punch at the whole
entourage. He spent most of the meal talking
enthusiastically about the ins and outs of training, while
Geoff responded with questions and interest. (Put on as
far as Petra was concerned, but then no one would have
cared to hear her opinion.)

Sunny might have known how Petra felt, but she was
clearly impressed with Geoff's background, his charm
and his second set of biscuits. (Petra tasted one,
acknowledged sourly that it was light and fluffy and
refused to finish it despite Sunny's severe look.)

And then there was Jennifer. Petra could have truly
done without Jennifer. She was just about as fluffy as
Geoff's biscuits. She smiled and giggled and simpered
and blushed. She wore her blonde hair in bouncy pigtails

tied with blue bows and was dressed in a one-piece playsuit whose brevity revealed a sexual development at thirteen that far exceeded Petra's at twenty-five. And she was oh, so helpful. Jennifer couldn't wait to be of use to anyone. She jumped up to help Sunny serve dinner and she passed the salt to Geoff with such a batting of her long, dark eyelashes that Petra almost gagged over her green beans. And everything, according to Jennifer, was 'neat'. The food was 'neat', the lake was 'neat', the cottage was 'neat', the swimming was 'neat', the trees were . . .

Petra's level of tolerance had hit such a low by the time dessert was served that she had to excuse herself from the table, saying she'd developed a terrible headache. That caused Sunny's mothering instincts to go into overdrive, and Petra was provided with anxious sympathy, aspirins, a cool cloth, a cup of tea and an extra blanket. She curled under the blanket, listened to the laughter and murmur of voices from the kitchen and decided that the month at Indian Lake was going to be far worse than she had even imagined.

Far, far worse.

CHAPTER THREE

GEOFF limped down the steps to the beach below the cottage, spread out the towel he had brought with him and sat down on it. He was wearing a brief bathing suit, a slip of dark silk, that exposed most of him to the caress of a breeze that played off the lake. He tucked the knee of his good leg under his chin, wrapped his arms around it and became motionless, letting himself absorb the warmth of the sun on his shoulders, the sound of water lapping against the shore, the light filtering through the branches of a nearby poplar to play with golden fingers on the blue surface of the lake. There was something extremely seductive about the beauty and serenity of his surroundings, and despite his angry words to Rick, Geoff was discovering that he wasn't really unhappy to be here. For the first time in months he felt himself relaxing; his chafing need to move, to hustle, to find the action evaporating into the very air around him.

It had been a long time since he'd felt so at peace. There had been the push to get through college, the urge to get a job and then the desire to get the plum of reporting jobs. After that, he'd spent time rushing from one place to another, from one interview to another, from one woman to another. Even when he'd been in the hospital, he'd spent so much time fighting the pain, he'd never truly rested. And he'd been so miserable during his convalescence that he'd never taken a moment just to sit, just to take a deep breath, just to let the world flow over him. It was different now to find himself in a place without telephones, newspapers, televisions and radios. It placed him in an enforced isolation that he had thought he would hate with a

vengeance. Instead, surprisingly, he had the sensation
that he was being held in a gentle cocoon, nourished by
the silence and an utter lack of urgency.

Geoff hadn't had any chance to talk to Petra yet. She
reminded him of a deer, shying away at any motion or
overture that he made. So he'd ignored her and
concentrated on other things like talking to Joe about
marathon swimming and helping Sunny cook. Geoff
knew he made a mean biscuit but that's about as far as his
culinary talents went. Under Sunny's tutelage he might
even attain such heights as yeast buns and coffee cake.
And there was, of course, Jennifer who had a crush on
him so intense that Geoff practically shuddered when
she came within reaching distance. God, but he'd
forgotten what teenage girls could be like. Those
yearning brown eyes, that awe-struck expression. Geoff
was almost afraid to speak because he could feel
Jennifer collecting his every word as if it were a precious
gem and tucking it away in her memory to taste and
savour later. And he had to walk a tightrope in his
treatment of her. He didn't want to hurt her feelings
but, on the other hand, he didn't want to encourage her
either. That was the other thing he'd forgotten about
teenage girls. They were sweet and pretty and
deliciously wholesome but, when they opened their
mouths...Geoff had heard Jennifer talking to Sunny
about him and had winced to hear himself described as
'really, really neat.'

Now, why couldn't Petra feel that way, he wondered.
That would sure make life easier for him. A little
adoration could go a long way in getting a reporting
job done. But he wasn't so lucky. Petra was turning into
one of the world's most elusive creatures. The only
times he could really watch her was when she was
swimming, and she seemed to do that for most of the
day. The rest of her time was filled up with meals,
walking Rembrandt, reading on the porch or sleeping.
She was civil to him, but only barely and, whenever he

was in the same room with her, he could practically feel her urgent wish to leave. He'd tried casual conversation, idle flirting, an easy smile. Heck, he'd even paraded his bathing-suit-clad body in front of her to see if she'd show a flicker of interest. No luck there either. It seemed that Petra Morgan was unmoved by a body that had inspired rhapsodies from other, far more attractive women.

Geoff grinned to himself. Well, so much for male egotism. Not that he was upset about her lack of interest. He still considered Petra as one of the least seductive women he'd ever met. What had Sunny said about her? All bones, that's what she was. Although . . . and he had to admit this . . . after watching her swim, Geoff had found himself with the urge to touch her, to test muscles that must be as hard as rock beneath the sleekness of her skin. And, if there was one thing that was truly beautiful about Petra, it was her skin. He hadn't noticed it at the pool where the fluorescent lighting made everyone look sallow, but here at the lake with the sun bathing her in a glow, he had noticed the colour of her; an amber that reminded him of honey. It was an odd combination with her dark hair and grey eyes, but it was pleasing, and he couldn't help wondering if she was like that all over.

A rustle of leaves behind him caused Geoff to turn, and he caught sight of Petra standing uncertainly in the trees behind him, a towel slung over her shoulder. He knew that she didn't want to come down to the beach because he was there, and she was already turning to go away when he said, 'Come on. I don't bite or, at least, I don't think that I bite. And I promise not to ask any questions.'

Petra turned back, stared at him for a second as if she were trying to decide just how impolite she could be and then capitulated with a small nod of her head. She walked out on to the sand and put her towel as far from Geoff as possible. This left them only sitting about three feet apart since Joe had never bothered to clear enough brush to make the beach anything more than a narrow strip of sand with a wooden jetty off it that pointed out to the middle of the lake.

Geoff watched as she neatly straightened her towel out and lay down on it, her arms at her sides, her face angled towards the sun, her eyes closed. Instead of wearing her usual one-piece stretch suit, she was dressed in a red string bikini, and Geoff quite enjoyed the discovery that . . . yes, Petra was a warm honey-amber from beneath her breasts, down the curve of her waist and across the flat expanse of her abdomen. That left only . . .

He shook his head and said, 'Aren't you training today?'

She didn't bother to open her eyes. 'That's a question.'

'Sorry, I'll rephrase it. You aren't training today.'

'I usually take one day off a week to give my joints and muscles a chance to rest.'

'Gotcha.' He was also quite entranced with the discovery that Petra did have breasts. Small, admittedly, but they were overflowing the top of her bikini in a very pleasing fashion. 'Hey, why don't you ask me questions? That would be a change of pace.'

There was a long silence while Petra seemed to make up her mind. Then she turned over on to her side, causing those very same breasts to make an enticing shift to the left and said, 'What happened to your leg?'

Geoff looked away from her watchful grey eyes and back at the sparkling water of the lake. A fish leaped in the distance, a cascade of diamonds swirling into the air. Nearer to shore, water spiders skated on the lake's surface making tiny circular ripples, and a dragonfly hovered past, its wings a gleaming iridescent blue. It was a scene that was idyllic and peaceful, a far cry from that day of screaming and pain and devastation.

Reluctantly, he spoke, 'I was stationed in Beirut and walked down the wrong street.'

Petra waited but it was clear that Geoff wasn't going to say any more. 'And then what happened?'

He supposed it was fair, her asking him questions that he didn't like to answer. But the fairness of the situation didn't make the reply any easier. 'A bomb went off that blew my leg apart and killed the guy next to me.'

'Did you know who he was?'

'No, but we spent several hours together buried under a building that had fallen over us. I guess you could say,' his voice was wry, 'that we did have a chance to get acquainted.'

'And then what?'

Geoff glanced at her. 'And then we were dug out and I was taken to a hospital where they attempted to put me back together.'

'Will you ever walk without a limp again?'

It was plainly and brutally put. Most people edged around that question, sidestepping the painful issue. Even his parents and brothers hadn't dared to ask Geoff if he was going to be a cripple for the rest of his life. His fierce scowl and obvious reluctance to talk about his leg had put everyone off except Petra. 'I don't know,' he finally said. 'Maybe.'

'That's too bad.'

But her voice was completely devoid of sympathy, and it made Geoff wince inside. It also made him wonder about his own interviewing technique. Did he come across as so uninterested? So carelessly probing? So idly curious? He had asked any number of people, including Petra, some hard questions. Some people were evasive, others were diplomatic, a few were even honest. But in his long and distinguished career, he'd never particularly cared how the questions had made his interviewees feel. The need to get the story had always been so strong that the end had justified the means, and he'd been willing to sacrifice anything and anyone to achieve it. Now, with the tables turned,

Geoff was finding that experience painful and un-pleasant.

For a long time, the two of them were silent. Petra had turned over so that she was lying on her stomach and Geoff was, once again, staring out across the lake. Then she spoke, 'Do you like it here?'

'Surprisingly, I do.'

'Why is it a surprise?'

'I thought I'd be bored.'

'I love it up here,' she said with more enthusiasm in her voice than he'd ever heard before. 'It's so peaceful and quiet.'

'Don't you like teaching?'

Petra hadn't seemed to notice that he'd done the forbidden and asked a question. She picked up some sand in her hand and let the grains sift through her fingers. 'I love teaching but when the school year is over, I'm just as glad to get away from school as the kids are. And then,' she added with her first smile of the morning, 'when summer's over I can't wait to get back.'

Geoff was quite struck by that smile. It was spontaneous and warm and happy, and he'd never seen Petra anything but cool and controlled before. Oh, she was affectionate with Sunny and Joe, but there was always a part of her that seemed to be carefully watching herself, monitoring her emotions, gauging just how far she should go. He wondered if she were different in the classroom where she was only being judged by the uncritical eye of small children.

'Well,' he said carefully, not wanting to alter the tentative peace between them and knowing he had to stay away from dangerous ground, 'I always hated school. I never wanted to go back.'

'Oh, one of those.'

'I was a terror in the playground, too.'

'Were you?'

'I was wild at times,' he said ruefully. 'I have this embarrassing memory of spitting in the water fountain to get a couple of girls mad. They told the teacher and I had to call my father and tell him what I did.'

'And that cured you?'

'Yup. Never spat in another water fountain in my life.' Petra had put her head down in her arms, but Geoff could have sworn that she was smiling. Encouraged, he kept on, 'Of course, being one of four brothers didn't make it easy. We were all rambunctious. We were always wrestling, fighting and playing tricks on one aother.' He paused, savouring a memory. 'I'll never forget what we did to Alex, my youngest brother, when he was about eight. He was the kind of kid who abhorred cleanliness. He never used soap in the shower and only brushed his teeth when stuff started to grow on them. Tom and I were babysitting him once, and we decided that he was going to have clean teeth, once and for all.'

'Uh-oh,' said Petra, turning her head to look at him. 'Poor Alex.'

'Yeah, we were pretty sadistic. We told him what we were going to do and dragged him bodily up the stairs to the bathroom. All the way, he kept screaming, "You can't make me!" "That's what you think," we told him. Anyway, we got him into the bathroom, forcibly held him down on the toilet seat, and pinched his nose shut. When he opened his mouth to breathe, zap! In went a heavily coated toothbrush.' Geoff took a quick glance at Petra, saw that she was actually laughing this time and went in for the punchline. 'The kid was lucky to have his molars left when we were done.'

'Oh,' said Petra, taking a shaky, laughing breath, 'the cruelty of children.'

'Of course, he squealed on us, the rat. We got him for that, too.'

'I didn't have any brothers or sisters.'

Her voice was wistful, and Geoff said, 'The grass is always greener. I spent years wishing I was an only child.'

Petra had propped her chin up on her hands and was staring off into the bushes. 'You would have hated it.'

He was careful not to look at her, not to make his voice seem eager or obtrusive. 'I don't know,' he said in a tone of idle speculation. 'Think of the advantages. One hundred percent of your parents' love and attention, not having to wear hand-me-downs, no one sneaking through your things and stealing your favourite toys.'

'It wasn't like that at all,' she said vehemently. 'It was . . .' And then she stopped, throwing a startled look at Geoff. 'Well, that was clever of you, wasn't it?' she added acidly.

'What?' His voice was innocent, but he knew what she meant, and he was thinking: damn and double damn.

Petra was sitting up now, bending over and hurriedly putting on her sandals. Her pose gave Geoff a clear view of curved amber breasts, lovely and soft. 'Don't ask the questions, but soften up the victim and she'll talk all day.'

'Petra, that wasn't what I . . .'

She stood up, her towel over her arm. 'But the victim isn't as stupid as you think,' she said coldly.

'I didn't . . .'

But she was gone, her sandals slapping against the bottom of her feet, punctuating the silence with an angry staccato sound. Geoff watched her figure disappear into the bush and then he stretched out on his towel, sighing heavily. He had thought that talk of his family was about as innocuous as he could get, but instead it seemed that he'd trodden on some dangerous territory. He could only surmise that there was something in Petra's background that made her so sensitive. Something that might or might not have to do with her swimming. Geoff curled his fingers into the sand and wondered how much he should dig to find out what it was. A good reporter would leave no stone unturned; a compassionate person would respect the fences that Petra had erected around herself.

Geoff spread his fingers and watched the grains of sand fall back on to the beach. Compassion wasn't one of his virtues, never had been. It was a quality that hadn't got much nourishment in his family. Oh, they all loved one another, he supposed, but in the rough and tumble of his childhood, it had been each boy out for his own. Mistakes weren't tolerated, clumsiness was ridiculed, and even the most momentary weakness could result in a loss of status in the family pecking order. The Hamilton brothers hadn't left much room in their lives for compassion.

And it didn't fit into his profession either. In fact, it would be an albatross around his neck. Compassion didn't generate great stories, wonderful scoops or penetrating interviews. Geoff had a reputation as a journalist who went for the gut, and he was proud of it. He'd never let compassion get in his way before, and the idea of tip-toeing around Petra Morgan's sensitivities and vulnerabilities thoroughly disgusted him. Geoff put his head down in his arms and thought that she'd be a fool if she expected him or any other reporter to be so understanding. Swimming Lake Ontario was a public event and a media affair. It made her fair game for the curious, the sensation-seekers and the celebrity hunters. He might not care a damn about the swim, but the rest of the world would want to know the whys, the hows and the wherefores of what seemed to most people to be an act of supreme torture. And if he didn't sift through Petra's life to find the clues to that swim, someone else would.

A good reporter would probe and dig and examine; a compassionate person would avoid the tender spots in Petra's psyche and walk carefully in a territory that was clearly explosive. But Geoff had never been one to shy away from danger. He'd walked into a booby-trapped street in Beirut, knowing full well that one small error in judgment could mean his death. And if the mistake meant that he would limp for the rest of his life? Well, the risks were part of the job, and they didn't detract from his enjoyment of it. Hell, they even added to the thrill of it all.

A good reporter or a compassionate man? Geoff flipped over on his back, closed his eyes and let the sun's rays warm his chest and face. It wasn't a choice that would leave him in agonies of self-doubt or caught on the horns of a two-pronged dilemma. All his life, Geoff had known precisely what he wanted to be.

The best damned reporter in the world.

Petra had learned early in life that she had a thing for animals and they, in return, had a thing for her. Dogs wagged their tails in ecstatic joy when they saw her, and they were apt to jump up on her shoulders, lick her face and follow her around. Cats were more restrained but equally affectionate in their own way. They crawled into her lap and purred. They liked to weave around her legs. Several cats of her acquaintance even went so far as to lie on their backs when she was around in the hopes of getting their stomachs scratched. And, of course, Petra gave in. She was one of the world's best tummy-rubbers, ear-scratchers and all-round petters that she knew. At least that seemed to be the consensus of the animals she knew.

Rembrandt and Renoir were no exception. Renoir had immediately deserted Sunny on the evening of Petra's arrival, and Petra had been awakened in the middle of the night to find herself nose-to-nose with a curious cat. When she'd sleepily turned over, Renoir had climbed up on to her back, stepped down into the valley created in the blankets by her bent knees and settled in for a nice snooze. It was all very comfortable and cosy except that Petra had been periodically aroused by Renoir who purred like a buzz-saw badly in need of repair.

Rembrandt, who slept outside, had taken to not only following Petra around on land but also pursuing her in the water. He usually accompanied her on at least one or two laps of her training swim. After that, he cheerfully flopped down on a rock by the shoreline and, lowering his great black head on to his paws, watched Petra until she was done. Then he followed her into the cabin where he hung around while she had lunch. And Petra always shared a bit of her meal with him, being totally incapable of resisting the appeal in those huge, brown and mournful-looking eyes.

'You're such a sucker,' Sunny said. 'Honest to Pete, that dog knows when he's latched on to a good thing.'

'I can't help it,' Petra said, munching on a ham sandwich that was missing most of its ham while Rembrandt was enjoying his share under the table.

Sunny was busy making an apple pie, rolling out the dough on to a floured board. 'You're so crazy about animals that I've always wondered why you didn't have a pet of your own.'

The question caught Petra unawares. 'Oh, I . . . well, it's my mother, you see.'

'She doesn't like pets?'

Petra looked down at her sandwich. 'No.'

Sunny was one of the few people in Petra's acquaintance who had actually met her mother and understood the family circumstances. Now, she glanced sympathetically at Petra's bent head and said, 'How many months has Sheila been in the hospital this year?'

'Five, so far.'

'And what do the doctors say?'

Petra gave an unhappy shrug. 'They don't say anything except that she's a chronic case and there isn't a cure for . . . what she has.'

'What *is* the diagnosis?'

'Depression, instability, mental illness, schizophrenia. Every doctor says something different, but it doesn't really matter what label they put on it. She's sick, that's all.' Petra took a bite of her sandwich, discovered that it had turned tasteless and passed it under the table to Rembrandt.

'Is there anything they can . . .?'

'She looks terrible, too. She's lost weight and she's very shaky. I don't know whether it's the drugs or what, but every time I see her, I get worried. But they tell me that she eats a bit, and she doesn't seem to be too unhappy, but how can I tell? It isn't as if she'll talk very much to me.'

'Oh, Petra.' Sunny reached over and put her floured fingers on Petra's clenched hands.

But the words wouldn't stop coming as if they'd been building up inside her and fighting to break loose. 'Sometimes, I'm not even sure she knows when I'm there. She stares at the wall or the ceiling or the floor. And she makes this peculiar little twisting motion with her fingers, over and over again.' To her horror, Petra heard her voice crack and felt tears dampen her lashes. It wasn't the first time she'd cried over her mother, but she had never broken down in front of anyone before. Quickly, she pulled her hands away, blinked again and gave Sunny a small, wavering smile. 'Anyway,' she added, her back quite rigid and her voice now held to a monotone, 'the flat's too small for a dog and the super doesn't like cats.'

There were any number of things that Sunny could have done then. She could have followed her instincts and taken Petra into her arms and comforted her. She could have offered her a Kleenex and tea and soothing words. But, if Sunny had any urge to supply Petra with the mothering she needed, she was smart enough not to show it. She carefully moved away from Petra and went back to her pie dough, pummelling it with an unusual show of fury. 'Well, there you are,' she finally said, clearing her throat. 'It was stupid of me to ask in the first place. Now, what are your plans for the afternoon?'

Silently thanking Sunny for the chance to regain her composure, Petra stood up and felt Rembrandt's wet nose sneaking into her hand. 'I thought I'd drive into town. Is there anything you need?'

'Mmmm—let's see. Milk, butter, fruit if there's anything available, Joe wouldn't mind a newspaper and some aspirin, please.'

'Sure.'

'Oh, and Petra? Take Jennifer along, will you? The child's suffering from cabin fever and has been begging me for a trip into Mercy.'

Petra glanced down at the dog at her feet. 'And I don't suppose Rembrandt can be left behind, can he?'

Sunny gave her a pleading smile. 'Poor Remmie would be miserable,' she said. 'He thinks a car ride is hid God-given right.'

Rembrandt occupied the entire back seat of her small Toyota. He liked to sit with his head out of an open window, his tongue lolling, his ears streaming in the wind. Jennifer sat in the front with Petra, who would have preferred her human companion to be as mute as her animal one, but of course she wasn't that lucky. Jennifer liked to chat during car rides. All the way to town, Petra was the unwilling listener to a long story about how the students in Jennifer's Grade 10 class read *The Merchant of Venice*, went to see it at the theatre and then acted out the parts themselves. That story, in turn, led to a description of Jennifer's English teacher (he's great), her best friend (we've been close since we were five, isn't that neat?) and her high school (divided between two cliques; the punks and the preps). Petra smiled, nodded and put in the appropriate word or exclamation when the situation seemed to demand one. But she was relieved when they finally reached town and she pulled into a parking spot.

'Here we are,' she said. 'And Toronto, it isn't.'

Jennifer glanced dubiously at the six shops that lined both sides of the dusty street, the pick-up van parked beside them and the one overhead traffic light that blinked yellow at periodic intervals and said, 'What do they call this place again?'

'Mercy, Ontario.'

Jennifer grimaced. 'As in "Have mercy on our souls"?'

For the first time, Petra found herself liking Jennifer. 'That's it,' she said with a smile.

Jennifer pointed to the drug store where a sign advertising a sale of bandages covered most of the window. 'Do you think they'll sell make-up?'

Petra looked at Jennifer's big, brown eyes, naturally pink cheeks and flawless smile. 'You want to buy make-up?' she asked. One of the best parts of a sojourn at the cottage as far as Petra was concerned was that such urban necessities as make-up and stockings could be ignored.

'Oh, yes,' Jennifer said. 'I really want to look a lot older.'

It took Petra one hour, three shops and four errands later to figure that remark out and then she winced. Jennifer's crush on Geoff seemed to be escalating. It had started with lovestricken looks, moved into shy attempts at flirtation and was now branching out into the realms of appearance. Petra couldn't help wondering how Geoff would feel when Jennifer approached him in full cosmetic regalia. Would he notice the thickened eyelashes, coloured mascara and lips glistening with newly applied lipstick? Or would he treat her with the same casual friendliness he'd managed for the past week? Petra had to hand it to Geoff for his talents in the how-to-handle-adolescents department. Jennifer's attempts to gain his attention were so blatant and so painful that Petra had wanted to take her aside, pat her on the head and explain the hard facts of life to her. Grown men of thirty-six were rarely interested in girls of thirteen and, if they were, one couldn't help thinking there was something peculiar about them. Jennifer needed to understand that boys wanted girls while men wanted women.

Men wanted women. The phrase brought Petra back to that morning two days ago when she'd joined Geoff on the beach. It was a memory that she had quite deliberately and successfully put out of her mind. It wasn't the conversation that bothered her so much any more, although she still was convinced that his efforts to get her to talk were underhand. No, it was something else that had hung in the air between them. She had felt Geoff's eyes on her breasts, assessing them and, for the first time, assessing her as a sexual being. She had known quite early on in their relationship that Geoff didn't find her attractive. Not that there was any concrete evidence to support that belief, but Petra had sensed that Geoff had examined her and found her wanting. It didn't bother her as much as it might have bothered another woman. After her bad love affair, Petra found his indifference to her more comforting than disturbing. She didn't want to attract men; she hadn't wanted Geoff to be sexually interested in her at all.

That was until she'd spent that morning with him and had noticed the way he was eyeing her, judging her and, for the first time since they'd met, finding her attractive. The impact of this sudden interest had its repercussions. Petra discovered that she was now uncomfortably aware of him; of his face, his gestures, the way he talked. To her horror, she had found herself dwelling on Geoff's body, seeing it as she had seen it that morning, stretched out on a towel, barely covered by a bathing suit, the sun turning the hair in his chest into bright filaments of gold. Not even the scar on his leg could detract from a physical presence that was masculine, highly attractive and extremely sexy. Petra had swum three miles during one training session and discovered that her mind had been quite filled by that body. It had taken extraordinary concentration to exorcise its image from her mind and every bit of will-power she had to suppress the sensations that image had aroused within her. Petra had, to her astonishment, wondered what that body would feel like against her, what it would be like to touch the muscles of an abdomen that was ridged in muscle, what it ...

Petra blinked, realised that she had walked out of the grocery shop and was already standing by the car. Rembrandt, who had been waiting for her on the pavement, was back at her side.

'Remmie,' she said with a bit of desperation, 'say something intelligent.'

Rembrandt looked up at her with adoring eyes.

'As a conversationalist, you leave something to be desired.'

His tail wagged.

'Christ,' she muttered to herself, opening the car's boot, 'talking to a dog. I must be going crazy.'

With the groceries packed away, Petra entered the drug store to find Jennifer standing at the cosmetics counter surrounded by bottles, jars and tubes while the assistant, a gentleman in his sixties, watched her with disbelief and bewilderment.

'What do you think?' Jennifer asked, turning to Petra. The brown eyes were surrounded by red and purple shades of shadow and heavily lined with black, her cheekbones were slashed with red and her lips were a deep purple. The look was quite incongruous with her pigtails, blue T-shirt and denim jeans.

'Well,' Petra said, aiming for tact, 'the effect is ... dramatic.'

Jennifer frowned. 'Too punk?'

Petra had to confess that she wasn't really into the subtleties of various 'looks'. 'But the colours seem ... well, a little strong for you.'

The assistant took off his wire spectacles, rubbed his balding forehead, and then put them back on. 'Just what I was saying to the young lady,' he said in a relieved tone of voice.

Jennifer took a Kleenex and began to wipe her eye make-up off. 'That's what my sister wears,' she said stubbornly.

'How old is she?'

'Twenty.'

'I see.'

'And a lot of guys think she's sexy.'

'Really?'

Jennifer looked sadly into the little stand-up mirror at the edge of the counter. 'She dates a *lot*.'

Petra tried another approach. 'Every woman has her own style, you know. I'd say yours would be soft blues, pinks, maybe a bit of lavender.'

Jennifer perked up immediately. 'You think so?'

It took half an hour, more experimentation and a thoroughly befuddled assistant before Jennifer was equipped with a base make-up, blusher, eye shadow, mascara and lipstick. As they drove back to the cottage, she chatted happily on about her family. She was the youngest with a brother and a sister and a neat cat named Missy and ... Petra drove, her eyes on the ribbon of road in front of them and tried to let the words roll over her. But it wasn't easy, and she wondered sadly if she was destined to spend the rest of her month at Indian Lake listening to other people tell stories about their parents, siblings and happy childhoods. She would nod and smile and, in Geoff's case, she had even laughed, but her laughter had been bittersweet, tinged with the sad yearnings of her own childhood, the silent prayers that God might bring her father back and the desperate wishes that her mother would be different.

Petra never talked about her past to anyone and, when she'd found herself close to revealing even a bit of it to Geoff, she'd pulled away as if she'd drawn too close to a burning fire. She hadn't dared, even for a moment, to let him glimpse at the agony that had been her childhood. For the first time in many years, Petra wondered why she was so reticent. Oh, it was true that Geoff was a reporter and might use that information in a public and embarrassing way, but he wasn't the only one she'd fled from. There had been other acquaintances who had tried to be friends; fellow-teachers who had wanted to draw Petra into their circle. And she had always resisted their warmth and their smiles until they left her alone. She'd resisted because she was frightened of . . . afraid of . . . what?

Petra's hands tightened on the steering-wheel. She wasn't the only child in the world who had grown up without a father or had a mother that was mentally ill. She hadn't been the only little girl on earth who had longed for a sister or a brother. Even her awkwardness with other people wasn't abnormal. The advice columns were filled with stories of unhappy individuals who didn't relate well to the outside world. What precisely was she hiding? The shame and embarrassment of the past? It was true that those emotions had been so strong that even now she could feel their power, but she was old enough to shrug them off. Her bad love affair? In this day and age, such liaisons were a dime a dozen. That's why Geoff had hit upon it at that breakfast. What man or woman in the free-for-all of the 1980s had not participated in a sexual encounter that was unsatisfactory or disappointing?

So, even though she felt she was different from other people, set apart from the mainstream of life by her past, Petra was intellectually ready to agree that she wasn't unique or special. Yet, she had never been able to confide in anyone. Something had always held her back from being more open, more honest, more accessible. Even when she wanted to speak, she found it difficult. Either she choked on her words the way she had with Sunny at lunch or the words would simply not come out, as if some barrier had been placed in their way.

'... and my brother is getting a degree in accounting,' Jennifer was saying. 'My dad's really pleased about that and ...'

It hit Petra then, that sudden realisation. Perhaps, she thought, she wasn't only hiding her past from acquaintances, friends and strangers. Perhaps there was more to her instinctive tendency to conceal things than she had ever imagined. Perhaps ... and this thought came to her with a sudden contraction of her heart ... perhaps she was also hiding something from herself.

CHAPTER FOUR

THE second Monday of their stay at Indian Lake began with a spectacular sunrise and a morning heat that promised to turn the day into a scorcher. It was also the Monday that their bad luck began but no one at the McGinnis cottage knew that. Everyone got up, had a light breakfast, did stretching exercises for a half-hour and then headed to the lake. Even Sunny thought she'd take a dip before the sun reached its zenith. The water, she claimed, was always at its nicest before noon when the winds usually sprang up, ruffling its placid surface. Petra also loved the lake in the early morning. It was the time of day before those living in neighbouring cottages were up and about. There were no children jumping off docks, screaming and splashing, and motorboats were still moored to jetties, their engines mute. The only sounds at the lake were the ones supplied by nature; the croak of a frog, the splash of a fish, the whizzing of an insect's wings as it flew by.

Joe broke the silence. 'Okay, folks,' he said. 'No standing around and wasting time. Let's hit the water.'

Joe liked to put on a military demeanour at the beginning of a training session. It was only one of his many façades as a coach. By the middle of a session, he was hoarse from screaming and was inclined to be negative.

'For God's sake, Petra, you'll never cross the lake if you don't put on the steam.'

By the end of the session, he could barely speak but his enthusiasm was overwhelming. 'A world record,' he would crow, 'you're going to crack the world record.'

Petra had learned to adjust to Joe in all his incarnations, and she had to admit that he had her all psyched out. She needed a push to get her in, a reminder of her goal around the twelfth mile when she couldn't care less, and a pat on the back when she got out.

Meanwhile, Sunny was giving Joe a look of disgust as she said to the rest of them, 'I love his language, don't you? "Hit the water." What does that mean?'

'He's trying to inspire us,' Geoff said wryly. Petra glanced at him as he flexed his shoulders and stood with his legs wide apart to keep his balance. She'd seen him swimming, but he hadn't joined them during a training session before. She hoped he knew what he was doing. Long distances were hard on muscles that were unaccustomed to the pace.

'That means,' Joe grumbled, 'that I want you in— and on the double. None of this chattering and yammering.'

Sunny rolled her eyes to the sky. 'Is he usually such a slave-driver?'

Jennifer grinned. 'He gets worse, Mrs McGinnis.'

Sunny groaned. 'Is that right?'

Joe ignored her. 'Petra, take the warm-up miles slow—about sixty strokes per minute. Jennifer, you're to stay with her. Don't get rambunctious. This isn't a race. Geoff, you swim by Petra's right side. You haven't tried this before so stick close to shore. Sunny . . .'

'Aye, aye, sir,' she said. Jennifer, Geoff and Petra exchanged smiles. Joe and Sunny had been married for thirty-five years and had developed a pattern of bickering and verbal sparring that barely concealed a comfortable intimacy and a great deal of affection.

Joe took his eyes off his clipboard. 'Sunny, my sweet, you're being insubordinate.'

Sunny fluttered her eyes at him. 'I wish you wouldn't say things like that in public, Joe. It's embarrassing.'

Jennifer giggled and Joe gave her a mock glare. 'Two extra lengths, Jennifer, for laughing at my wife's rotten jokes.'

Geoff patted Jennifer on the shoulder. 'It's okay,' he said. 'Joe forgot his whip today.'

'That's enough!' Joe roared. 'In!'

Petra was smiling as she walked into the lake. The water felt lovely and cool against her skin, and she pulled down her cap and adjusted her swimming goggles so that they fitted snugly around the orbits of her eyes. Beside her, Jennifer was doing the same, the muscles in her arms bunching as she adjusted the strap. Petra was now used to swimming with Jennifer and she had to admit that the girl had the potential to be a fine racer. She certainly had the build for it, wide shoulders and long muscular legs. And she had a lovely crawl stroke, streamlined, rapid and efficient. She'd had some trouble learning to slow herself down to Petra's pace for the initial four miles of swimming, but now she could do it beautifully. And, when it came to the sprinting miles, Jennifer could beat Petra hands down until they hit the eight-mile point. After that, she began to flag, finally dropping out when they'd done ten miles. Petra was on her own after that, swimming mile after mile until she reached twenty. Today, Joe had put a new wrinkle into her training. He'd decided that Petra should spend her seventeenth mile swimming in her sweat suit. 'You'll feel like you're flying on the eighteenth,' he'd said. Petra had no doubt that she would. She also wondered if she'd sink before she reached that marvellous condition.

'Any time you're ready,' Joe said.

Petra glanced at Jennifer who nodded and then at Geoff. She'd been avoiding him again and he'd known it. She'd made sure that the only time they were together was when someone else was around, and she'd caught him watching her, those blue eyes of his clear but unreadable.

'Ready?' she asked.

His grin back was easy, jaunty. 'Any time you are.'

Petra dived into the water then and felt rather than

saw Jennifer and Geoff dive in beside her. Within
seconds, she had automatically fallen into that
accustomed sequence; head turning over and over
again to the left, arm after arm pulling steadily
through the water, legs in a smooth flutter kick. It
was as natural to her as walking and, within minutes,
she had entered that other world, that cool blue place
where nothing mattered but the rhythm and the pace.
She began her swim as she began all of them, by
reciting the Greek alphabet to herself. *Alpha, beta,
gamma, delta, epsilon, zeta, eta, theta* ... she had
memorised it when she'd discovered that the letters of
the English alphabet weren't enough of a challenge
... *psi, omega* ... She had reached the other shore, a
distance of one quarter-mile and, putting her foot
down, turned and pushed off the lake bottom. *Alpha,
beta, gamma* ...

One quarter-mile merged with another and then
another. By now, the alphabet had eased Petra into that
state of mind where she was floating nowhere, thinking
of nothing, existing outside time and space. It was in
this frame of mind that she could swim for hours and
for miles. It was this mind-set that made her a long-
distance swimmer for, without it, she wouldn't have
been able to stand the monotony or the boredom. She
had once read somewhere that marathoners swam in a
state of sensory deprivation. Their skins were usually
numbed by the coolness of the water and their senses of
sight, smelling and hearing were inhibited by goggles,
ear and nose plugs. There was nowhere for their minds
to go except into some other dimension. Petra couldn't
have told anyone exactly where or what that dimension
was. She could only describe it as a place where the
hours felt like minutes and miles seemed to pass by in a
few strokes.

The sound of a whistle penetrated her consciousness,
and Petra came out of her reverie to find herself
instinctively speeding up. She and Jennifer were now in

a sprint, racing one another. Water splashed on her goggles as Jennifer sped ahead of her. Petra moved even more quickly until she was just behind the other girl. The extra power that she had came from hours and hours of swimming and a body that had been trained to call upon hidden reserves when they were needed. Without the ability to tap the strength lying latent in her muscles, Petra knew she wouldn't have a chance of crossing Lake Ontario. The conditions wouldn't be optimum then, not as they were today with the sun shining and the water smooth, warm and placid. She'd be swimming in the black of the night against waves that would bat her from side to side. And the winds of the lake were known for their capriciousness. They could come up out of nowhere, beating the water into a frenzy and causing its temperature to drop until she would be forced out or suffer hypothermia.

Joe blew his whistle again and Petra slowed down, once more swimming at her former warm-up pace. She had reached the far shore, turned and started again when there was a frantic splashing at her side and a hoarse cry. She came to an abrupt stop and pulled herself into an upright position to find Geoff flailing beside her.

Petra tore off her goggles. 'What's the matter?' she asked.

'Cramp,' he said, panting. 'In my leg.'

'Roll over,' she said, 'try to massage it out.'

His face was twisted with agony as he turned over, floated on his stomach and tried to knead out the cramp under water.

'What's going on?' Joe hollered, his voice echoing over the lake, and Jennifer's figure swimming towards him.

'Cramp!' she yelled back and he ran towards the boat that was moored to the dock. Geoff's face came up out of the water. 'Is it gone?'

He shook his head, the pain making him mute. It had

also drawn his mouth into a grimace and caused his breath to come in short bursts.

Petra moved closer to him. 'Can you make it to shore?'

'Don't know.' The words were expelled between clenched teeth.

'We're not far,' she said. 'I can tow you in.'

He nodded again, but only barely this time as the pain caught at him again, forcing his head down.

Petra swam swiftly towards him, put her hands on his shoulders and, silently thanking those instructors who had drilled life-saving techniques into her, easily turned him on to his back. Then, cupping his chin with her hand, she began to swim, using a strong scissors kick and a powerful pull with her right arm. Geoff was heavy but the buoyancy of the water enabled her to go at a steady pace. She talked to him all the while. 'I've got you now ... take it easy ... we'll be there soon ...'

'Christ,' he breathed.

'Hold on.'

As soon as Petra could touch bottom, she towed him into the shallow water. He crawled from there on to the beach and then curled up on the sand, his hands around the upper part of his injured right leg. Petra dropped down beside him and put her hands on his thigh.

'Let me try,' she said.

But the muscle, the one at the back of his leg, had gathered into a knot so hard and so contracted that Petra could not even begin to ease it. She'd once had a cramp herself and that had been in the sole of her foot. The pain had been absolutely excruciating, curling her toes up in agony. She could imagine what Geoff was feeling in a muscle that was ten times larger and that much more powerful. Finally, her fingers came to a rest and she said helplessly, 'I'm sorry, I can't ...'

'That's okay,' he muttered. She leaned over him to see his face and felt her heart twist at the sight of him. In his agony, he had dug his head into the sand and clenched his eyes shut. Grains of sand were caught in his eyelashes and eyebrows and adhered to his skin where it was wet. Gently she brushed them off and felt the roughness of his beard beneath her fingers and then, as her hand moved to his temple, the springing dampness of his hair. He was starting to sweat from the pain now and beads of perspiration dotted his forehead. There was nothing Petra could do except hold him close to her and pray for Joe to hurry. Kneeling beside him, she curled her arm over his chest and placed her cheek against the skin of his back. She could hear his heart thudding and, beneath the hand that lay on his chest, she could feel the quickened pace of his breathing. Without realising what she was doing, Petra gently caressed the broad planes of his torso, his body hair catching in her fingers.

'Where's the cramp?' Joe had arrived and, leaping out of the boat, ran up on to the beach.

Petra sat up. 'His bad leg,' she said.

But not even Joe's experienced hands could release the spasm. By this time, Sunny had shooed Jennifer back up to the cabin and had then driven around the curve of the lake in the car, and they were able to half-carry Geoff up on to the gravelled road and then lay him down in the back seat.

'Let's take him into town,' Joe said. 'He's going to need more than an aspirin and a heating pad for this.'

Petra held Geoff's head on her lap as they bounced and jolted their way into Mercy. He moaned once but otherwise kept his teeth clenched so tight that she could see the ridge of muscle in his neck and jaw. His eyes were closed too, and Petra did the little bit she could to help him. Over and over again she rubbed his temples in half-circles and then ran her fingers back through the hair over his ears. The texture of it was different from her own silky strands; it was coarse and thick, a dark-gold where it was wet and a silvery gold where it was dry. It curled around her small hands and, unconsciously, she tugged gently on it, enjoying the feel of it between her fingers.

Joe pulled with a screech up to the small brick building that was Mercy's hospital. Within minutes, Geoff was out of the car, on to a stretcher and being pushed into the emergency ward. Joe, Sunny and Petra sat in the tiny waiting-room with towels over their bare shoulders. In the rush of the moment, they had left the lake clad only in their bathing suits.

'I shouldn't have let him try that swim,' Joe said. 'His leg wasn't up to it.'

'You couldn't know that,' Sunny said. 'He'd been doing so well.'

But Joe was still upset. 'Too much, too soon,' he muttered to himself.

Petra tried to bury herself in a tattered old *Ladies' Home Journal*. It was a Christmas issue from three years before, and it was almost impossible for her to maintain an interest in tree decorations and gingerbread houses. Finally, she gave up, drew the towel tighter around her shoulders and leaned her head against the wall at the back of the chair. Closing her eyes, she tried to eliminate Geoff's face from her consciousness, but that was impossible, too. Now that the crisis was over, now that Geoff was under the responsible care of a capable medical staff, Petra was remembering with astonishment and not a little embarrassment the way she had acted when he was hurt. She had not been able to keep her hands off him. She had touched, handled, stroked and caressed a man that she professed to dislike intensely as if . . . as if she desired him.

Petra opened her eyes and stared down at her traitorous hands with their narrow palms and small, delicate fingers. She didn't do much for her hands except to put lotion on them to keep the skin from drying out after so much exposure to water. Her nails were short and unpolished and she never wore rings. Her hands were bare of ornamentation and tanned now from exposure to the sun: the hands of a woman who rarely gave them any thought but who, in a most unconscious way, used them to express tenderness, affection, love.

Petra flexed her fingers and realised that she'd never understood that before, had never realised that what she couldn't articulate in a verbal way was spoken silently by her hands. She'd often touched her small students at school, brushing the hair back from their eyes, patting them on the head, holding their hands in her own when she was trying to make a point. And then there was her affinity for animals. She loved to hold them and pet them, small furry beasts that, in their mute way, sensed what those caresses meant and returned her affection with an unqualified enthusiasm and undemanding love.

Petra had always thought of herself as cold, as aloof, as unaffectionate. Her mother had once sadly told her that she was as distant as a stranger; her ex-lover had accused her angrily of having ice running through her veins. And Petra had believed them because she'd had no other relationships that she could use as a mirror to reflect who and what she was. Sunny and Joe's affection had been so unconditionally offered to any swimmer that came under their supervision that Petra had never counted their feelings towards her as realistic assessments of her personality. What she had believed was that she was unlikable and unlovable except by children, animals and other helpless creatures.

'Oh,' she said and Sunny looked up.

'What?'

'Sorry, it's nothing,' Petra said and closed her eyes again. Was it so surprising then that she should offer to Geoff, in his most helpless moment, some of that care and tenderness? It had nothing to do with the fact that he was a man and she was a woman. His body was attractive, yes, but her reaction was not what she feared. She hadn't fallen over into the terrifying abyss of infatuation or sexual interest. No, instead she had bestowed upon him gestures that were natural to her, instinctive. Yes, that's what they were, she thought with a sense of relief, an instinctual response to a being who was hurt and in distress. And, of course, he wouldn't remember anyway. He'd been far too involved with pain to notice anything that she had done. Petra took a deep breath and relaxed, letting her head once again rest against the wall. Everything would be just the same as it had been before, she thought complacently, all the pieces of the world held within their rightful place.

It was a belief that she was able to hold to until it blew up in her face. What Petra had quite forgotten in her frenzy of rationalisation had been the enjoyment, that wonderful pleasure, *she* had got from touching Geoff. That forgetfulness should have been no surprise; she'd spent a lifetime training herself to conceal her true feelings behind façades, explanations, and abstract reasoning. It was a habit that would take a strong man and a great deal of love to break. But that was in the future.

Geoff came out of a deep sleep and, for a moment, wondered where he was. Then he noticed the ceiling made of boards, the logs that made up the walls and the primrose-printed curtains that Sunny had hung on the window of his bedroom. The late afternoon sun filtered through the rose and cream fabric, its rays low and angled. He shifted slightly in the bed, felt the ache in his leg and remembered. With a sigh he lay back and felt the old despair return. Hell, but he was tired of being sick, of hurting, of limping, of finding himself hemmed in on every side. His world had contracted since the accident. He couldn't jog, he couldn't hike, he couldn't go dancing, he couldn't assume any more that he had the stamina and ability to try even the simplest of physical activities. All he had done this morning was swim, a few more lengths than he was used to, that was true, but look where it'd got him. Flat on his back, convalescing once again. *Damn*.

And he'd almost drowned. The muscle had cramped and the pain had bent him double. He understood now how people could actually die in the water from abdominal cramps. When a muscle as strong as the stomach went into a knot, the swimmer wouldn't have a chance. He, at least, had been able to straighten up occasionally. Well, two painkillers and one cortisone shot later, and he was once again fit to join the human race. Not that he'd be without pain. The muscle ached now, unremittingly. He hated like hell to take drugs, but he supposed he'd have to take another pill in order to sleep tonight.

There was a tentative rapping on his door and he said, 'Yes?'

'Are you awake?'

Geoff had the urge to ask how he could have answered if he were asleep, but he recognised the anxiety in Jennifer's voice and didn't have the heart to hurt her feelings. 'Yes,' he said.

The door opened and she peered around its jamb. 'How are you feeling?'

'I'll live.'

'Oh.' She was in the door then, carrying a tray that held a steaming cup of tea and some slices of Sunny's lemon bread. 'I brought you something to eat. I mean, you've been asleep for *hours*, and I thought . . .'

Geoff took pity on her. 'It's all right,' he said. 'I am hungry.'

'Oh, good.' Jennifer smiled brilliantly at him and placed the tray on his dresser. 'If you sit up a bit, you'll be able to eat.'

Geoff pulled himself up slightly, holding the sheet to his bare chest so that it wouldn't slip down. He was naked beneath the sheets and, from the way Jennifer had glanced at him and then shyly looked away, he saw that she had guessed at his condition. God knew what kind of fantasies *that* would generate in that overheated adolescent imagination of hers. Geoff tried to envisage what went on in the female teenaged brain and then gave up. On the other hand, he could sense her palpitations from three feet away. He cursed to himself, but offered her a pleasant smile as he accepted the mug from her outstretched hand.

'I hope you like Earl Grey,' she said.

'Love it.'

'Do you? Oh, me, too.'

It figured.

'And the lemon bread is delicious,' she went on. 'It really is.'

Geoff stared down at the plate she put on his outstretched legs. 'Thanks.'

'Of course, Sunny thought you might want something . . . well, more substantial, but whenever I'm not feeling well, I like tea and cake.' She gave him a worried glance. 'Don't you?'

'My favourites.'

Jennifer gave a happy sigh. 'I knew it,' she said as she perched at the foot of the bed, crossing her bared legs. She was dressed in her usual outfit, a T-shirt that was too tight for her and a pair of denim jeans. Her blonde pigtails were adorned with their blue bows.

It occurred to Geoff that Jennifer was in the early stages of becoming the kind of blonde he'd been accustomed to taking out. She certainly had all the equipment: curves, long legs, big brown eyes, and a conversational patter that was eminently forgettable. He took a sip of the tea, a bite of the bread and then, as the slanting sun caught her face, stared at her in growing horror. What on earth had she done to her face? Pancake make-up was spread so thick on her skin that she looked as if she were wearing a mask. Her eyelashes were so black and mascara-laden they could have walked of their own accord, spider-like, across the floor. Her cheekbones had been slashed with red, and her mouth . . . Jesus, that wasn't 'hot pink'—the colour was so vivid, it was practically at the boiling point.

But Jennifer, oblivious of his horrified stare, was chatting on in her usual fashion. '. . . and they brought you back from the hospital and you couldn't talk. I mean, you were muttering and mumbling to yourself. And you looked terrible, sort of white. Joe practically had to carry you in here.'

This wasn't the kind of information that Geoff particularly wanted to hear so he diverted Jennifer by asking her about her afternoon swim when she and Joe worked on her strokes.

'I'm working on my left arm,' she said. 'It's lazy.' And then she launched into a technical discussion of streamlining, efficiency and water friction. It interested Geoff that, when she talked about swimming, Jennifer suddenly became pragmatic and mature. When he'd first met her, he'd thought Joe was crazy to take her on; Jennifer hadn't seemed like champion material. But she was a phenomenal swimmer, and she took her talent seriously, training willingly and with enthusiasm. The only trouble was that, when she wasn't talking about kicking techniques, stroke rates and sprint times, she reverted right back to her thirteen-year-old self.

'The tea and cake were great,' Geoff said, handing his cup and plate to her. 'Thanks for thinking of me.'

Jennifer was all smiles. 'Oh, I didn't mind,' she said. 'And I'll bring you dinner, too.'

'No, thanks.'

'Really,' she protested. 'I'd *love* to.'

That's precisely what Geoff was afraid of—hours of Jennifer, hovering over him, studying his every expression, wanting to talk to him, trying to pamper the life out of him. He saw that he was going to have to nip this nurturing instinct in the bud.

'I've got to get up now.' Geoff pushed down the sheet slightly so that his navel was now visible.

Jennifer's eyes grew wide with alarm. 'But, I . . .'

The sheet went down another half-inch. 'Nature calls, sweetheart.'

'Oh!'

Geoff had never seen such a quick exit in his life. He was still grinning as he divested himself totally of the sheet and swung his legs to the side of the bed. The ache in his muscle intensified to the point that his grin was erased. It was a moment before he could stand, and another moment before he could hobble, carefully, over to the dresser where he pulled out a pair of jockey shorts, jeans and a T-shirt. Dressing was slow and painful. Geoff indulged in several pointed remarks that would have made his mother blush had she been around to hear them. As it was, no one was witness to his colourful vocabulary or the excruciating process by which he got his clothes on. Which was just as well, because his weakness and his trembling would have embarassed the hell out of him.

After dinner Geoff sat out on the screened porch on a chaise-longue. Sunny had fussed over him, putting a blanket over his knees, a cup of coffee at his elbow and a pile of novels on the floor for him to read if he got bored watching the sun set over the lake. Renoir, who had a yen for the chaise-longue, was curled up in a silvery grey ball at his feet. Joe and Sunny had taken Jennifer into Mercy so that she could call her parents and see a movie, while Petra had gone for a walk down at the edge of the lake. Geoff, therefore, had the cabin, the porch and the view on his own, but he wasn't particularly enjoying them. He was bored, restless and disgruntled with his own company. What he would have liked to do was go to a party where there was plenty of food, liquor and women, but his choices were far more limiting. There was the sunset, a novel or his own thoughts. Geoff opted for a book and picked up the nearest paperback. From its cover a man dressed in olive army clothes and with a machine-gun stared out at

him. Behind the man was a smoke cloud, a collapsing
house and people running off into the distance. Shades
of Beirut, Geoff thought with a shudder and, putting
the book down, picked up another one. A couple in
eighteenth-century clothes grappled on the front cover.
Geoff judged that the man was winning the wrestling
match because the woman's bodice was ripped open to a
point just short of indecency.

He stared at it for a moment, speculated on the
woman's half-hidden breasts and then leaned back on
the chaise-longue, closing his eyes and wondering when
the hell he was going to get laid again. Geoff wasn't
used to going without sex for long periods of time, but
the pickings at Indian Lake were mighty slim by
Hamilton standards. Sunny was a nice but married
lady, Jennifer was jail-bait and Petra was ... hmmm,
well the truth was that Geoff no longer looked upon
Petra as a female with the sex appeal of a wet paper bag.
He didn't know whether his tastes were changing or
whether abstinence makes the heart grow fonder or
whether there wasn't just something about her that
added up to more than the apparent sum of her parts.
She wasn't voluptuous or beautiful or sexy or ravishing.
She wasn't flirtatious, and she was impervious to any
vibes or signals that he gave out. He rather suspected
that Petra Morgan's sex life was a big zero, a goose egg,
zilch. But there was something about her that ... well,
intrigued him.

Geoff felt Renoir shift on his ankle as he pondered
the ethics of sleeping with an interviewee. All sorts of
complications could arise. His own reporting would be
coloured by the emotional dust raised during an affair.
His perspective would be tainted, altered, and distorted.
He might grow sentimental or, if the affair crashed on
the rocks, vindictive. No, Geoff thought regretfully, it
wouldn't do to get intimately involved with the subject
of his next feature article. He'd just have to suppress
natural urges and inclinations, put a lid on his libido, tell

that unruly part of his body to switch itself into neutral for the next few weeks. Then, when he returned to Toronto, there'd be females galore. There was even Marnie if he was so desperate that ... damn, how crazy could he get? Marnie. That would be like jumping from the frying pan into the fire. Marnie. Christ.

There was a squeak as the screen door moved on its hinges and Geoff opened his eyes. Petra was back from her walk with Rembrandt trotting alongside her.

'Sorry,' she said. 'I didn't mean to wake you.'

'I wasn't sleeping.' He smiled at her. 'Sit down and share the sunset with me.'

Geoff had thought she would refuse, but Petra sat on the wicker chair beside him and looked out of the screened window. The sun was sinking over the far edge of the lake, its golden half-circle reflected in the surface of the water as if it were a vast, gleaming mirror. Above it, the sky had turned to purple, its scattered clouds the colour of rose. Within half an hour, when the sun had finally disappeared, the dome above them would be a velvety black dotted with glittering, silver stars.

'It's pretty, isn't it?' she asked.

'I thought you'd watch it out on the jetty.'

'The bugs were starting to bite,' Petra said.

'And the mosquitoes around here are as big as fighter planes.'

She smiled. 'You're sounding better.'

'I thought I sounded okay at dinner.'

She shook her head. 'You were groggy.'

'Was I?' Geoff shook his head. 'Damn pills.'

'Is your leg still bothering you?'

He shrugged. 'Only a bit.'

There was a companionable silence for a while, and Geoff stole a glance at Petra. She was looking out at the sunset with an abstracted air, her hand idly stroking Rembrandt's head. Her hair curled around her head like a dark, gleaming halo and he noticed, for the first time, how pure her profile was. Like a Botticelli painting or the face on an ivory cameo.

Geoff cleared his throat. 'A penny,' he said.

Petra's turned shy. 'They're not even worth that much,' she said. 'In fact, I wasn't thinking much about anything.'

Her unexpected ease with him encouraged Geoff to move one step closer to intimacy. The tack he took, however, was seemingly innocent. 'I tried to read some of these,' he said, waving his hand at the pile of books, 'but I couldn't get into any of them.'

Petra glanced down at them. 'Are you a reader of fiction?'

'Rarely. I like biographies, history, that sort of thing. What about you?'

'I've never been much of a reader. I don't know why.'

'Do you like movies?'

Petra shook her head. 'I don't go to movies very much either. That's weird, I know.'

Geoff shook his head. 'Sometimes, I find movies hard to take. The stories are too painful or something. Or maybe I see too much real pain to want to watch it on the screen.'

'That's odd,' she said musingly, 'I've often felt that way myself.'

His voice was low, seemingly casual. 'Really?'

'It's all so phoney, you see. Those people up there or in books. They're artificial and their stories are artificial. The reality is so much worse that no author can imagine . . .'

'Can imagine what?'

The look she now gave him was cool now, less friendly, suspicious. 'Oh, no,' she said, 'not again.'

Geoff sighed. 'Petra, I don't ask you to talk about anything.'

'But you're dying to analyse me, aren't you? That's what this conversation is all about, isn't it?'

'Actually,' Geoff said easily, refusing to rise to the

bait, 'I hadn't thought about it, but now that you mention it—sure I would. You know, the motive behind the marathon or something like that.'

'Why can't you accept the fact that I'm just doing it for the challenge? People want to dive to the bottom of the oceans because . . .'

'Hold it,' Geoff said. 'I'll agree that there is something intrinsically appealing about challenges like that, but why doesn't everyone take them on?'

Petra shrugged. 'Because people are different.'

'Because,' Geoff said, 'certain people have a need to prove something to themselves.'

'Like what?'

He paused for a moment, trying to organise his thoughts. 'Perhaps they have to prove to themselves that they're courageous or, if they're doing something truly dangerous, perhaps they're fighting off a fear of death. Sometimes I've wondered if people who set themselves the challenge of conquering a natural obstacle aren't trying to control their environment in some way. I don't know exactly, but it seems too simple to me to say that just because a mountain's there someone will want to climb it.'

'You're reading too much into it,' Petra said hotly. 'That's the trouble with pop psychologists. They don't know what they're talking about.'

Geoff refused to get angry. 'And it also strikes me as a . . . well, self-centred endeavour.'

Petra was wary. 'What do you mean—self-centred?'

'Personal challenges don't add to the cause of humanity, do they? They just satisfy the person involved.'

If Geoff thought that he could further provoke Petra into talking about why she wanted to swim Lake Ontario, he was mistaken. She immediately went on the attack, making the obvious leap from Geoff's abstract discussion to herself. 'I don't know why you're covering this story,' she said coldly. 'You obviously think that marathon swimming is a waste of time.'

'I never implied that.'

'I can see the kind of article you're going to write,' she went on, her voice rising. 'You'll trivialise everything I've done, the hard work, the sacrifices, the hours of training. Is that why Allied Press put you on this story? So you could make fun of what Joe and I have done?'

Geoff sat up straighter, dislodging Renoir from his ankles and the cat leaped down to the floor. He hadn't let Petra's jibes get to him; he had very deliberately remained calm in the face of her growing anger, but now irritation began to seep in as she questioned his professional ability and integrity. 'I came to this with an open mind.'

'Like hell you did. You didn't want the assignment, you told me that yourself. What you really want to do is be back in Beirut getting shot at and reporting on man's inhumanity to man. That's what you journalists are after, isn't it? Sensationalist stories that invade other people's lives and poke into people's miseries and . . .'

That was coming too close to the bone. Petra wasn't the only person who thought that the media capitalised on tragedy and destruction, and Geoff was highly sensitive to such sorts of criticism. His irritation gave way to a barely controlled anger. 'At least,' he said, 'what I've reported on is meaningful.'

'Meaningful? What's meaningful about being on the outside and looking in? You have your nose pressed up to the window, peering in at events that happen to other people. You don't actually do anything. You just watch.'

Geoff's jaw was clenched. 'That's enough.'

But Petra was on a roll now, an angry, outraged roll. 'And you know something else? I've just figured out why you think that what I do is worthless. Because you can't swim more than half a mile without requiring medical aid. Because you're jealous.' Geoff felt the words rather than heard them. They were sharp and pointed. Like knives. Like claws. 'Because you're crippled, that's why, and jealous of me because *you* can't do what *I* can!'

Petra felt the words race out of her mouth at a speed so great that she couldn't call them back, think about them and, at her leisure, decide whether they were true or honest or fair. Instead they rushed out into the faded evening light to give the porch a sudden, horrifying clarity. For the first time, Petra noticed the miniscule hole in one corner of the window screen, the sliver of wicker that was unravelling on the arm of her chair, the pulse beating in Geoff's temple. He had gone quite rigid and there was a whiteness to the grim set of his mouth that let her know that she had gone too far. He didn't look directly at her. He had turned his head away as she had spoken and appeared to be studying the arc of sun that now rimmed the horizon of the lake like a curved gold band.

Petra stood up and clutched the edge of the wicker chair. 'I'm sorry,' she said. 'I didn't mean that.'

'Didn't you?' His voice was quiet, controlled.

'No. It was a ... thoughtless thing to say.'

'You sound as if you've thought it for a long time.'

'No, no, I haven't. It just popped into my head.'

He was silent then, still not looking at her, but his back was so rigid that Petra had the overwhelming urge to touch his shoulder, to stroke the hard muscles below his skin, to soothe away that tension. The urge was so strong that she had to physically clench her hand into a fist to stop it from moving forward. Instead, she used her voice. 'Geoff,' she said. 'I ...'

'And I suppose it's true,' he said, his tone flat and unemotional. 'I hadn't looked deep enough; I hadn't thought ... but I should have seen it. Jealous.' He paused and then spoke again, the bitterness sharp in his voice. 'Yes ... jealous.'

CHAPTER FIVE

ON the following Wednesday, Renoir disappeared. No one noticed until evening when she didn't return from her day-long hunting trip. Unlike most felines, Renoir was not nocturnal, a screw-up in her instincts that Joe attributed to the way Sunny had fussed over her as a kitten. Sunny, on the other hand, claimed that Renoir was probably not a cat in the true sense but a reincarnation of royalty. For example, Renoir adored olives, shunned cheap cat food for ground-up steak, and always assumed that the best chair in the house belonged to her. But, whether she was cat or queen, her striped black and grey form was always apparent around dinnertime when the food pickings were good and in the later evening when she liked to roam from person to person, bestowing on them, in a regal fashion, the pleasure of her company.

But on Wednesday night, Renoir didn't appear for dinner and wasn't underfoot that evening when everyone was seated in the central room of the cottage. Petra was mending a pair of shorts, Jennifer was reading a *Teen* magazine and Geoff appeared to be asleep with his head back on the couch, his foot propped up on an ottoman. The only lively spot in the room was the rummy game going on between Sunny and Joe. They played every night, keeping score on the back of an old grocery bill and totting up the winner at the end of the week. It was a game that involved intense competition and a great deal of verbal sparring.

'A deuce?' Sunny said with disgust as Joe placed a card on the discard pile. 'Is that the best you can do?'

'For you, love of my life. It's all for you.'

Sunny had put on her glasses and was now peering at

her hand. Her hair, piled up in its usual untidy bun, was threatening to slip off her head and she'd stuck several combs on various parts of her skull to keep it in place. She sniffed and said, 'You're so generous.'

'That's what you always tell me.' Joe also wore glasses when he was reading and playing cards. He rubbed his crew-cut with his hand and then drummed his fingers on the table. 'Come on, sweetheart. You're dawdling.'

'Dawdling!? Well, I'll dawdle if I want to.'

'It's against the tournament rules.'

'Tournament,' Sunny said with a sniff. 'You call this a tournament?'

At that moment, Geoff lifted his head and Petra lifted hers. Their eyes met, acknowledging a secret amusement at Sunny and Joe's continuing repartee at rummy. Then he put his head back and closed his eyes again. Petra heaved a silent sigh of relief that he was being friendly again. There had been hours since their conversation on the porch two days ago when Geoff would neither look at or talk to her. He hadn't been obtrusive about it, and Petra didn't think anyone else at the cottage noticed his animosity, but she had felt it and knew that it was deserved.

She had struck out at Geoff blindly and uncaringly and, whether her words had hit home or not, she'd felt guilty ever since. Of course he couldn't swim the way she did. He couldn't walk as fast either or dance the night away or climb trees. For the rest of his life, Geoff would have to limp and Petra, who was in prime condition, her body capable and responsive to whatever she wished to inflict upon it, had unthinkingly thrown her health in his face. It was one of the ugliest things she'd ever done, and she'd hated herself ever since. But there hadn't seemed any way of making the situation better. She couldn't take back the words or try to alter them. She couldn't change the fact that her limbs were sound and Geoff's were not. She had wanted to apologise to him, but the right moment had not presented itself, and Petra had found that she was too shy to seek him out.

Sunny picked up the deuce, put it in her hand and, after long deliberation, put down a black queen. 'Has anyone,' she asked, 'seen that damn-fool cat?'

Jennifer looked up from her magazine. 'I haven't seen Renoir since this morning.'

Joe gave Sunny a look of sneaky triumph. 'I've been looking for this lady,' he said, picking up the queen.

Sunny gave a groan. 'I thought you were saving kings.'

'That's for me to know, and you to find out.'

'Blast.' She stared pensively at her hand and then said, 'It isn't like her to be out after dark.'

'She's probably heading home right now,' Joe said, 'on a beeline for her bottle of olives.'

'Or,' Geoff said, 'she has taken to star-gazing and moon-watching.'

'I'm getting worried,' Sunny said.

'You should be,' Joe said with a smug satisfaction. 'I've got rummy.'

But by morning, when Renoir had still not appeared, Sunny was really concerned. She got up at six and, having taken a box of Puss N' Boots Nibbles out of the cupboard, circled the outside of the cottage, shaking the cat food so that the Nibbles rattled inside and calling out, 'Here, Renoir. Come on.' When no cat appeared she looked in and under the cars and then went further into the trees, peering through bushes and looking around logs. Rembrandt followed her around, looking perplexed, his tail giving sporadic wags while his eyes rested on the box of Nibbles. Rembrandt liked cat food almost as much as he liked his Fido Burgers.

When her searching and calling had failed, Sunny returned to the cottage looking unhappy and distracted. By that time, everyone else had got up and were in the midst of preparing breakfast. They tried to reassure her that Renoir would return by reminding her that cats have nine lives or suggesting that Renoir had met a lover out in the woods.

'She's never stayed away this long,' Sunny said.

'Give it another day,' Joe said soothingly. 'If she isn't back by then, we'll beat the bushes for her.'

'But she could be anywhere,' Sunny said, and they all knew what she meant. There was miles of uninhabited territory around Indian Lake.

Petra knew how much the animals meant to Sunny and put her hand on the other woman's shoulder. 'I'll take the car after my swim and drive around the lake. Maybe she's just lost.'

But Sunny was too upset to listen or to watch what she was doing. With an abstracted air, she took one of her homemade loaves of bread down from the breadbox over the wood stove, put it down on the cutting-board, picked up a knife and then, with a slicing motion, almost managed to cut off her left thumb. Blood spurted in a miniature geyser out on to the tablecloth, the bread, the knife and the cutting-board. Sunny made a gasping sound, went absolutely white and abruptly sat down, all the while staring at her hand. The others were frozen for a second, but then Joe and Geoff moved quickly. Joe wrapped a cloth around her thumb, pressing tightly to stop the bleeding while Geoff pushed Sunny's head down towards her knees.

Petra had taken one glance at the blood, Sunny's waxen face and then rushed into the bathroom to get the first-aid kit which was stored in the cabinet. It was a large blue box with a red cross on the cover and, when it was opened, displayed a wide assortment of bandages, medicines, splints, and needles. One time, Petra had read the manual that came with it and discovered that, with this kit, it was possible not only to set broken bones and bandage cuts but also to assist at a cardiac arrest and deliver babies.

But when she returned to the kitchen, she found that Joe had decided that their own emergency first-aid

LOVE IS A DISTANT SHORE

equipment wasn't enough. Sunny was resting her head on his shoulder, her eyes were closed and her face was screwed up in pain. Joe, who had gone ashen beneath his tan, was saying, 'I think she's going to need stitches.'

Geoff had taken hold of Sunny's hand and was holding the makeshift bandage tight against the wound. 'It looks pretty bad.'

'We'll have to take her in to the hospital.'

'Yes,' Geoff said. 'I'll go and get the car started.'

Jennifer, who had watched the entire proceedings with a hand held to her mouth, now jumped up. 'I'll go with you,' she said.

Sunny opened her eyes and, despite the pain and a pallor that was extreme, tried to joke. 'Think they'll recognise us at the emergency room?' she asked.

'Why not?' Joe said, tightening his arm around her shoulder. 'We made a big impression last time.'

No one wanted to remain at the cottage, but Sunny insisted that someone stay in case Renoir returned. So Petra watched the four of them drive out in Joe's big Chevy, gazing at the road until the dust raised by the speeding car disappeared. Then she heaved a sigh and went back into the cottage where she set about cleaning up the kitchen. She thought about Geoff's injury, Renoir's disappearance and now Sunny's accident and wondered whether the summer was jinxed. Not that Petra was superstitious. She never carried lucky pieces or worried about black cats or walking under ladders or thought that Friday the 13th was different from any other day. She didn't believe in ESP or ghosts or a preordained fate.

No, she never been superstitious, and she realised that she'd grown up believing that life was nothing more than a series of chaotic events that could or could not bring a person happiness. If you were born into the right family, then you were fortunate enough to be successful and content. If, on the other hand, you grew

up, as she had done, in half a family with a sick mother
and not enough money, then life was going to be rough
and difficult. She had always accepted this and
understood that she could take nothing for granted.
Not good luck or happiness or success. It was, she
supposed, one of the reasons why she worked and
trained so hard. In her heart, Petra knew that she
couldn't trust anyone or anything to help her achieve
what she wanted. The burden of success had always
fallen completely on her.

For the first time, Petra began to understand why she
was so fiercely independent. Oh, she knew she'd been
forced into a solitary role by her mother, and she'd
always been shy, but neither of those facts was reason
enough to account for an avoidance of personal
relationships that verged on the pathological. Petra had
turned her back on women friends and ran from men.
Except for that regrettable lapse into an affair, she
hadn't cultivated any acquaintances. She'd thought her
hands-off attitude arose out of pride and self-reliance
and shyness but now she saw that fear was another
component. If she dared, even for a moment, to let
down her guard, Petra might find herself relying on
another human being, leaning on that person, needing
and clinging to someone in order to survive. And, deep
inside, she was afraid, terrified even, that the person she
chose would turn out to be like her mother, another
Sheila, another weak link that snapped the minute
things got tough.

Petra wiped off the table and thought sadly of the
child she'd been and the lessons she'd learned. They
hadn't been nice ones; they hadn't been the ordinary
learning experiences of most children. Life had taught
her that the world was a jungle in which only the fittest
survive and that, in that jungle, love had no meaning,
no place and no function. It couldn't feed her, support
her or protect her from the harsh realities of economic
and familial failure. Petra looked back at herself as a

child and saw a little girl carefully picking her way
through debris in a terrain that was pitted, barren and
ugly. Was it any wonder that she had learned to be
aloof and suspicious? Should it come as any surprise
that she had no lovers and, apart from Sunny and Joe,
no friends either? Or that, inside, she was empty, alone
and, despite all the barricades she'd erected around
herself, still afraid?

Looking that deep within herself made Petra feel
dizzy and unhappy. It was far preferable, she thought
with a wry irony, to skate along the surface of life and
ignore the cracking ice below her feet. She finished
cleaning up the kitchen and then tried to relax on the
porch with a mystery novel and a cup of coffee. But
what was preferable wasn't always easy, and Petra
found that the mystery novel couldn't absorb her and
her coffee tasted flat. So she decided to go for a brisk
walk in the morning air, clear her mind and search for
Renoir. Picking up the box of Nibbles, she opened the
porch door and was just about to step out, when a grey
and black form streaked into the cottage, through the
main room and then into her bedroom.

'Well,' she said, putting down the Nibbles and
smiling to think how happy Sunny would be. 'So you've
decided to come home.'

But there was no answering sound from the cat and
her triangular face with its amber eyes didn't appear in
the bedroom doorway. Petra frowned, walked into the
main room of the cottage and then noticed the drops of
blood on the floor. At first, she thought they must have
come from Sunny when she cut her thumb, but then she
saw something more ominous. The drops formed a red
trail across the floor and over the sill of the doorway.
She realised with horror and a sinking heart that the
blood came from Renoir.

'I don't believe this,' she said in despair to the empty
room and the uninhabited chairs. A headache was
gathering itself at the edges of her skull; she could feel

the pressure begin to build at her temples. 'I really don't believe this.'

Petra took a deep breath, walked into her bedroom and, kneeling on the floor, put her head down so that she could peer under the bed. Her eyes had to adjust to the darkness there, and it was a while before she could see the cat sitting on its haunches under the furthest corner of the bed. She could barely make out Renoir's shape; all she could see was the golden gleam of the cat's round and unblinking eyes.

'Come on, Rennie,' she said. 'Come on out.'

But coaxing like that had no effect, so Petra went back into the kitchen and filled three bowls; one with water, one with olives and one with Nibbles. She brought them into the bedroom, put all three beside her on the floor and, once again, looked under the bed.

'Food, Rennie. Olives and Nibbles. Yummy and delicious.'

But that didn't work either and, no matter how much she coaxed and begged, Renoir wouldn't budge. She merely stared at Petra's anxious face as if she'd never seen her before. Petra finally gave up and leaned her aching head against the edge of the mattress, wondering how badly Renoir was injured and what she was going to do. There was no moving the bed in her tiny room without moving the dresser first. And, even if she did shift all the furniture around trying to reach Renoir, nothing would stop the cat from scurrying to another corner before Petra could get her hands on her.

Finally, in desperation, she got a broom out of the closet and used it to push the bowls deeper under the bed. In a few seconds, she was rewarded with the sound of a cat lapping water and she gave a small sigh of relief. Then she went back into the kitchen, got out the Mercy phone book, found the address for the nearest vet and jotted it down on a piece of paper. After much searching, she located the cat carrier, a wooden box with a mesh door at one end and put it on the kitchen table. Then she began an internal debate. Should she drive into Mercy, go to the hospital and get someone to come back and help her with the cat or should she wait in case Renoir did emerge? She wondered how bad Renoir's injury was and how much she was bleeding. She worried about the fact that if Renoir did start moving again she might bleed even more. She fretted until the aching in her head developed into a full-scale pounding and she had to press her hands to her temples in an effort to stop the pain.

By this time Rembrandt was scratching urgently at the back door and whining until he got Petra's attention. She opened the door, let him in and said, 'Now what?' Rembrandt licked her hand and managed to look both anxious and pleading at the same time. Petra sighed and fondled his velvety ears.

'Right,' she said. 'Lunchtime.'

She was in the midst of opening a can of dog chow when she heard a car drive up to the cottage and, looking out of the window, saw that it was Geoff in the Chevy. Petra didn't think she'd ever been so happy to see someone in her life; by this time, she couldn't have cared that he was a detested journalist snooping in the details of her life. He looked absolutely wonderful to her as he stepped out of the car, his blond hair gleaming in the sun, his face tanned and handsome, his lips curving into a grin as he caught sight of her.

Trailed by an eager Rembrandt, Petra ran out of the cottage. 'How's Sunny?' she asked.

Geoff's grin disappeared. 'Not good,' he said grimly.

'Why? What's happened?' Petra had a horrible vision of Sunny laid out on a hospital bed, her eyes closed, her thumb gone.

'She fainted and they've decided to keep her overnight.'

'And her thumb?'

'That's going to be okay although the doctor told Joe it might have limited movement after it's healed.

Petra let out her breath. 'Oh.'

'Anyway, I've come back to get some . . .' But then Geoff noticed that Petra was still looking alarmed and was now wringing her hands together so hard he could hear her knuckles crack. 'Is something else the matter?'

She nodded. 'It's Renoir.'

'Renoir?'

'She's under my bed and bleeding and I can't get her out.'

Two hours later, Geoff and Petra emerged from the vet's office. The cat, the doctor said, had been attacked by some animal in the bush. She'd had severe lacerations from being clawed and puncture wounds from being bitten. She'd required fifteen stitches and a shot to ward off infection. And she was spending the night in the animal hospital so that she could be watched. The vet hadn't been willing to pinpoint what kind of animal Renoir had come up against, but he ventured a guess at a racoon or fox. He didn't think the wounds had been caused by a bear, he'd said, the teeth marks were too small. Petra's mouth had dropped open when he'd said that. She'd never given a thought to what kind of larger animal life was roaming the bush just beyond the boundaries of the McGinnis cottage. Bears struck her as particularly dangerous, but the vet had smiled at her expression and reassured her that they rarely attacked humans.

Now, as she got into the car, Petra thought back on the afternoon and wondered if she could tolerate one more out-of-the-ordinary event. It had taken them an hour to get Renoir out from under her bed, an hour of moving furniture, removing sheets and blankets, closing the bedroom door and then upending the bed so that the cat had nowhere to go. When Petra had finally picked her up, Renoir had half-heartedly tried to wriggle away, but the sticky, matted fur on her belly, the pool of blood on the floor and the torn flap of one ear had testified to the severity of her injuries. She'd even willingly sat on Petra's lap, wrapped in a towel, as Geoff drove into Mercy. Rembrandt had been the only one who'd objected. They'd fed him lunch and then locked him in the cottage. When he'd realised that they were going to leave in the car, he'd begun howling his abandonment so loudly that Petra could hear the noise over the revving of the engine as they drove away.

'Well,' said Geoff, as he glanced back at the vet's office, 'that's one patient safely in bed.'

'Who's next?' Petra asked.

'Next? Oh, you mean who's going to get pneumonia or fall down and break a leg?'

Petra nodded. 'I'm not superstitious but this is getting ridiculous, isn't it?'

Geoff walked around to his side of the car. 'They say bad luck comes in threes, but I'm not superstitious either.' He grinned at her over the bonnet. 'Still, I think I'll stay away from sharp knives, cliffs, guns and land mines.'

They drove the mile to the hospital and parked in its car-park. Petra took Sunny's overnight case out of the boot and, closing the boot door, straightened up just as Geoff began walking towards the hospital entrance. For a moment, she watched him and, being sensitive after the horrible things she had said to him, noticed just how bad his limp really was. He still needed the cane to keep his balance, and he couldn't pull his full weight on the bad leg. This combination of problems meant that he was forced to go slowly and to weave slightly from side to side. And it wasn't easy for him either. As she hurried to join him, Petra could see Geoff clenching his jaw and the gleam of perspiration on his brow. It occurred to her that Geoff was not only crippled but, quite possibly, in pain a great deal of the time.

The thought of it made her feel such an agonising pity for him and shame for what she had said, that

Petra wanted to apologise right there on the spot. 'Geoff . . .' she began.

'Hey,' he said, giving her a lop-sided grin. 'You don't have to wait for me. I'm a little slow.'

That made her feel even worse. 'Oh, no,' she said. 'I don't mind.'

But she did; she minded horribly for him that he should be reduced to this, to this crawling pace up the hot pavement. She didn't know how he could stand it, to have been reduced from whole to less than what he was, to know that for the rest of his life he would never walk or run without a limp again. Petra thought about her own exuberant good health and finely honed muscles and wondered how she would react if she lost her ability to swim, to move any way she wanted, to walk straight and tall.

For the first time, she saw Geoff in a new perspective. She couldn't imagine the horrors that he'd been through, buried under the rubble of Beirut and believing in an imminent death, but she was struck by his courage. A lesser man might have died; a lesser man might have faced diminished physical capabilities with fear, with depression, with a bitterness that ruined his life. But Geoff had done none of these things. He was back at work, trying his damnedest to get a story out of her. And Petra had the suspicion that the only reason he was at Indian Lake was that his boss wouldn't send him back to Beirut with a bum leg. She guessed that Geoff would have wanted to return and plunge right back into the danger that had cut him down; facing once again the chance of being shot or buried alive, of crippling another limb, of losing an eye or, ultimately, of losing his life. That took more courage than Petra had ever known.

As they entered the hospital, she admitted with reluctance that she had changed her mind about Geoffrey Hamilton. Quite against her will and her instincts, she had found that she admired him and even

liked him. He was still a journalist and her feelings
about journalists remained, but the man was not just
his profession. He was nice, charming, attractive and
kind. His concern over Sunny was genuine; he hadn't
hesitated to help with an injured cat. And Petra had
discovered that Geoff was easy to get along with, an
amiable man when they weren't arguing over their only
bone of contention—her. She glanced at his profile as
he held the hospital door open for her and suddenly
wanted to know more about him. She found herself
wondering what women he had dated and what love
affairs he'd had. It wasn't hard to guess that, with his
looks, Geoff would have rarely spent time alone. Yet,
Petra rather suspected that no woman had tied him
down for long. Geoff had been a rolling stone,
gathering no moss, no attachments, no clinging females
that would slow down his energetic pursuit of life.

They found Sunny in bed, tired but out of pain. Her
thumb was bandaged and she still looked white as the
sheet she lay on, but she smiled when she saw Petra and
lifted her injured hand. 'Welcome to my new domain,'
she said gaily.

Petra leaned over and kissed her wan cheek. 'How
are you feeling?'

'Fine. I don't understand why they're keeping me
here overnight. I hate hospitals.'

Joe was sitting at the edge of the bed, holding on to
Sunny's good hand. 'It's for your own good.'

'My own good,' Sunny snorted. 'Wouldn't a decent
night's sleep in my own bed be for my own good?'

'It wouldn't be for mine,' Joe grumbled. 'Don't want
a fainting female on my hands.'

Sunny gave Joe as much of a dirty look as her
exhaustion permitted. 'You're just worried about your
rummy game.'

'Ah!' Joe said with disgust. 'That'll be the day.'

Petra sat down on the other side of the bed. 'Fighting
again, are you?'

'Bickering,' Sunny said. 'We don't call it fighting. Now, did that dratted cat ever show up?'

Petra glanced at Geoff who was standing in the doorway. 'Well,' she said, 'Renoir did make it back but . . .'

'But . . .?' Sunny demanded.

'She's spending the night at the vet's. It seems that she ran into a fox or a racoon and needed a few stitches.'

Sunny shook her head in disbelief and then gave them a small smile. 'Well, we can convalesce together. Now, won't that be cosy.'

Petra, Geoff and Joe stayed and talked with Sunny for a while, but it was soon evident that whatever drugs she'd been given for pain and shock were having their effect. By the time they left, Sunny was asleep. They picked up Jennifer at Mercy's only dress shop, stopped at Mercy's only restaurant for hamburgers and finally headed back to the cottage where they found that Rembrandt, frantic in his isolation, had torn apart one of the decorative pillows on the couch. There were bits and pieces of foam on the surfaces of the furniture and on the floor. When they walked, the foam lifted and sifted around them like an indoor snowstorm. Joe held a severe conversation with Rembrandt, but the dog's look of shame only lasted for a few seconds. He was so ecstatic at their return that he followed them around, licking their hands and wagging his tail so hard that his rear end appeared to be gyrating.

Joe returned to the hospital for the evening visiting hours while the rest of them set about cleaning up the cottage and putting Petra's bedroom back in order. By the time Joe returned at ten o'clock, the cottage was clean, Rembrandt was fed and everyone was drooping with fatigue and heading for bed. By ten-thirty the lights were out, and the faint rumble of Joe's snoring could be heard through the cottage. Petra stretched out in her bed, trying to ignore the ache in her legs and the pounding in her head. Her headache had waxed and waned all day, easing to a vague aching before returning to a full pitch of pain. She wasn't used to having headaches, and she didn't know what to do about this one. It didn't respond to aspirin, to darkness or to the cool, wet cloth she'd placed on her forehead. Even with her eyes closed and her body very still, it rampaged through her head, beating angrily at her temples, clawing at the back of her eyes and tightening an iron band around her forehead.

When she could stand it no longer, Petra got out of bed, pulled a terry-cloth robe over her nakedness and slipped out of the door into the porch where the air was cooler. She had intended to stretch out on the daybed that had been built into one corner of the porch and let the night sounds wash over her, but when she got to it and put a hand down, her fingers didn't make contact with the bed's corduroy cover. Instead, her hand touched flesh.

She gave a little cry, but a male voice said, 'Shush, you'll wake everyone up.'

'Geoff!' she whispered. 'What are you doing here?'

'The same as you probably.' She heard a rustling and then he said, 'Here, sit down.'

Petra obediently sat on one end of the bed. Her eyes had become adjusted to the moonlight, and she could see Geoff's shadowy figure in the other corner. He was wearing shorts, but nothing else. Every once in a while a stray moonbeam would play over him, turning his shoulders, face and hair to silver. 'You couldn't sleep either?' she asked.

'Nope. My leg is bothering me.'

His voice was matter-of-fact so Petra merely said, 'Oh, I'm sorry. Does . . . does that happen often?'

'What—my leg? Only when I spend a lot of time on it—like today.'

Petra sighed. 'It was a hard day. Between Sunny and Renoir . . .' and her voice trailed off.

'And what's keeping you up?'

'Me? It's my head. It's pounding.'

'Did you try aspirin?'

'It didn't work.'

'Mmmm—I could probably fix it.'

Petra glanced suspiciously at his shadowed face. 'You could?'

'Sure.'

There was a silence that reverberated in Petra's head like the clanging of dissonant bells. The pain was so bad she put her hands to her head. 'How?' she asked.

'Lie down on your back and I'll show you.'

'Lie down . . .?'

'Assume the horizontal, face up, head in my direction.' His voice, despite its whisper, was clinical and commanding. 'Come on. It won't hurt.'

Petra found that she would do anything if it promised her some relief. Obediently, she lay down so that her head was by Geoff's legs. The next thing she felt was his hands on each side of her face, his fingers warm and taut as they began to smoothly massage her skin. Geoff could barely see what he was doing, but his hands saw for him. They felt the delicate line of her jawbone, the angle of her cheeks, the orbits of her eyes, the tender skin at her temples. With care and gentleness, his fingers moved on her until her tension slowly eased. Petra relaxed, closing her eyes, letting the hands move her head to one side and sighing gently when they soothed the rigid tendons on her neck.

'That feels good,' she said. 'When did you learn how to do that?'

'I had a girl friend once who had taken a course in massage. She taught me what she'd learned and we used to give each other massages.'

'That sounds heavenly.' And erotic. Despite her headache, Petra felt a sudden warmth at the thought of a man and a woman together, naked, hands on each other, easing, touching, stroking.

'It was.'

His hands were on the back of her neck now, digging deeply into the spasm of muscle. Petra sighed. 'Why'd you ever give her up?'

'Well, I don't actually remember giving her up. It was more like a mutual parting of the ways.' His voice held a wry note. 'To tell you the truth, I don't even remember her name.'

'Oh.'

'But I sure remember those hands.'

It was a while before Petra spoke. 'It sounds as if you've had a lot of girl friends.'

'I've had my share.'

'But not to remember the name of one . . .'

Geoff sighed and his hands dug into her hair, soothing the tensed muscles of her scalp. 'It doesn't reflect well on my character, does it?'

'Well, it seems sort of . . .' Petra sought the right word, 'casual.'

'Yeah, well, that's the way it's been. Casual. Easy come, easy go. I haven't had much time in my life for anything else.'

If Geoff was trying to sound nonchalant, he wasn't succeeding, because Petra caught a sad note in his voice. 'Why?' she asked.

His hands stopped moving for an instant and then started again. 'Because I was roaming the earth and writing stories. I never had much time for women, and my work was dangerous. I didn't want to inflict that kind of life on someone else. My risks were my own responsibility.'

'That makes for a lonely life.'

'It hadn't felt that way until . . .' His voice trailed off, hesitant and unsure.

'Until what?'

'Well, this sounds, I don't know, weak or something, but I hadn't felt lonely until I injured my leg.'

'Why is that weak?'

'Because ... because it implies that I only need someone when I'm ...' he gave an uncomfortable little laugh, '... half a man.'

That touched her. 'I don't think of you as half a man.'

'No?'

'You can do a lot of things—drive, swim ...'

'Not like you can.'

Petra tried to sit up but his hands firmly held her head down. His fingers were in her hair now, massaging her scalp. 'Geoff, very few people can swim the way I can. A lot of men couldn't do it. You mustn't judge yourself against me.'

His voice was low. 'But you were right, you know. I am jealous, damned jealous of you.'

'Geoff ...'

But she couldn't stop him. 'When I tried to swim with you and got that cramp, it came home to me that I was never going to be the same again. I think before that I'd always believed that one day the injury would disappear and I'd walk again, just the way I'd done before. I thought I'd start with swimming, it seemed easy enough, so I did a mini-training when you weren't around. I swam a couple of lengths, I did some exercises that Joe recommended. But it didn't work the way it would've in the past. The moment I tried to keep up with you, I discovered how wrong I had been. I'm a cripple, Petra. You were right about that, too.'

'I didn't mean to say those things, I've regretted them ever since. Geoff ... I've hated myself. Please ... I'm so sorry.'

His voice was oddly detached. 'Don't be sorry for the truth.'

'But it was said in anger.' Petra now pulled herself upright so that she and Geoff were looking at one another, their faces pale ovals in the moonlight. 'I really don't believe what I said.'

He spoke without self-pity, only the resigned

detachment of a man who has come to grips with the very bottom of despair. 'Petra, I'll never walk right again. I'll never . . .'

Her hands moved to his shoulders, her fingers tightening against his skin, urgent with the message in her heart. 'I don't know how to convince you,' she said. 'I admire you, I . . . respect you for your courage.'

'Courage?' he said disbelievingly.

'Yes.'

'You don't know,' he said with intensity, 'how I have raged and cursed. You don't know how I've cried.'

'Geoff, you're not a cripple or half a man. Not to me.'

'No?'

It filled her then, the need to tell him, to show him, to express to him what she had come to believe—that he was more a man than many she had known, that there was a wholeness to his spirit that had nothing to do with the injury to his flesh, that his jealousy of her was nothing compared to her jealousy of him. Petra desperately wished that she could be like Geoff. Brave and charming, eminently likable, unafraid of people, the kind of person who fitted in wherever he went. So, forgetful of the rigid hold she kept on herself, forgetful of that third, repressive eye that kept a watch over what she did, Petra leaned forward and brushed her lips against Geoff's, a gentle kiss, a comforting one. A kiss that said, please, please, believe me.

Geoff was motionless, still, hardly breathing.

His lips had felt soft, softer than she would have ever thought it possible for a man's lips to be. The skin of his shoulders was sleek and warm, the muscles hard under her fingers. Without speaking, she allowed her hands to move as they wished, the palms settling downwards so that they slid slightly lower to the winged bones of his shoulderblades. With the thumb and forefinger of each hand, she tracked the bones inward to their meeting place at the base of his throat. There, she felt a pulse beating, his lifeforce drumming beneath the sensitive tips of her fingers, its power crossing her own skin and bone, moving rhythmically into her blood, slowly altering to match her own quickened heart. And then, drawn forward by that twinning of blood-beat and pulse and breathing, Petra once again brought her mouth to his.

CHAPTER SIX

GEOFF had come out on to the porch, feeling sorry for himself, for the pain in his leg, and hating that damned sensation of self-pity that overcame him when he was tired or low or vulnerable. He had thought to lie down on the couch and listen to the night sounds through the screen; he, the urban man, had found an unexpected consolation in nature. The croaking of frogs and the buzzing of insects, the patter of rain on leaves, the scratching of a squirrel on the roof forced him to contemplate his own insignificance in the realm of things. The world ran on without him at the helm; it ran on without his participation in its daily events. It was humbling to think of himself in that way, and it was a novelty to see himself as just a small player in the natural cycle. One hundred years ago, Geoffrey Hamilton didn't exist and no one had cared; one hundred years from now, Geoffrey Hamilton would be dead and no one would care. It was an interesting contemplation for a man who had felt himself important to the way the world operated.

He saw now how deeply his arrogance had run, a river cut right into his soul, his personality, his temperament. He'd made assumptions about life that he thought were true and acted accordingly. He'd thought, for example, that he was invincible and had walked recklessly down a Beirut street that he'd known was dangerous. He'd thought the news couldn't be reported without him, but today when he'd been in the hospital, he'd picked up a newspaper and read the wire service clipping on the Middle East with Brennan's byline. It had been precise and competent, but he hadn't written it. He'd thought that his future was a line heading straight into further glory and renown, only to discover that nothing was fixed, certain, predictable.

Nothing was predictable. Not the day with its tragedies and disasters or the evening with its surprises. He hadn't expected to see Petra after she'd gone to bed, he'd been surprised to find himself talking to her about things he'd never breathed to another soul. And, when she'd kissed him the first time, with a spontaneity that, for her, was dazzling, he'd been stunned into stillness and silence. He had barely dared breathe as she moved her hands on his shoulders. In fact, he had stopped breathing, or so it seemed, when her fingers had moved to his throat where only the strong beat of his pulse gave away a growing excitement.

For a second, the world seemed to have stopped as her face turned once more upwards towards him. In the dimness of the moonlight, he could barely see the wondering eyes, the lips slightly parted. And then she had kissed him again, and the silence and stillness was broken. With a murmur low in his throat, Geoff pulled her towards him, his mouth widening hers, their tongues meeting in a heady, liquid touch. She wore a terry-cloth robe, barely cinched around her waist and, as he brought her up to his chest, the cloth parted so that the silky warmth of her breasts was against him.

No, nothing was ever predictable. Geoff had once thought Petra skinny and unattractive, convinced that he wouldn't have taken her if she'd been the last woman on earth. Then he realised that she was interesting and even enticing, but he'd decided that the desire to make love to her arose more out of frustration than anything else. Now, he was discovering that he wanted her. He wanted the touch of her, the taste of her, the feel of her. He cupped her face in his hands and explored her mouth, the corners of her lips, the tips of her eyes. He pushed back the shoulder of her terry-cloth robe and ran his thumb down the back of her, feeling the bumps of her spine, the delicate indentations of her ribs. He slid both hands to the front of her, and his palms stroked the hardened nipples of her breasts.

The sensation was intoxicating, and he brought his mouth down to her breasts, feeling Petra's hands digging in his hair as his head bent before her. Her skin tasted good, a salty, honey taste all rolled into one. With his mind's eye, he could imagine the colour of her in the sun; brown, amber and gold. He remembered the sight of her breasts moving in her bikini and his idle contemplation of the terrain below. Her breasts were no longer enough for him. Needing her, wanting her, his mind whirling with the sensations of her, Geoff pushed Petra backwards, his hands slipping lower down her body, testing the angled hipbones, the swirled navel, the concavity of her stomach and coming to rest at that focal point, that soft, wonderful juncture between her legs.

'Geoff . . . Geoff . . .'

It was a while before the whispered words made an impression on him or the hands pushing against his chest had any effect. It was a while before he could surface from his sexual haze into the reality of the dark night, the wind rustling in the trees outside, the hard edge of the bed beneath his legs. Shaking his head as if to clear his mind and taking a deep breath, Geoff pushed himself off her and sat up, rubbing his hand through his hair and willing his heart to slow its beat, his body to come to rest. For a few minutes in time, he had totally forgotten who he was, where he was or who he was holding in his arms.

There was a rustle of fabric as she pulled the terry-cloth robe around her and the faint sound of her quickened breathing. 'God, Petra,' he said. 'I'm sorry. I didn't mean that to happen.'

'It was my fault.'

'No, no, I got carried away.'

'It was my responsibility.'

'Petra, I . . .'

Her voice was breathless, shaky. 'I shouldn't have kissed you.'

Geoff felt her starting to stand up and he reached for her, grabbing her by the wrist. 'Why shouldn't you have kissed me?' he asked.

Petra sat down heavily. 'I didn't mean to. It was accidental.'

'I liked it.'

'No.' Her face turned towards his, her voice tremulous.

'And I liked you and the feel of you.'

'Geoff.'

'And I'd like to do it again, a little bit slower maybe and with more finesse and without Jennifer and Joe in nearby bedrooms.'

She tried to release her wrist from his grasp. 'Please,' she whispered.

Geoff sensed her trembling even before he pulled her into his arms, this time cuddling her close to him, tucking her head under his chin, wrapping his arms around her so that he could rest his hands on her clasped ones. She trembled like a bird caught in a trap, a wild animal held against its will. He silently cursed the passion that had risen in him and the celibacy that had let it loose to rampage through him so violently that he'd forgotten everything but his need for a woman. Petra was elusive prey, the kind that required quiet, unseen stalking and only the gentlest touch.

'Now, listen,' he said. 'We mustn't let ourselves worry about what happened tonight. It was a natural sort of thing. A man and a woman alone together, half-naked, in the moonlight. Hell, we're even a cliché.'

'It scared me,' she said, but he could feel her relaxing. The trembling was gone, and she was even leaning back against him. His lovemaking might have frightened her, but Geoff knew that she had liked it.

'Can you consider it a compliment? Like I was overcome with your charms?'

Petra cleared her throat. 'I thought that maybe you were . . . horny.'

A laugh rumbled in his throat. 'Petra Morgan, what an unladylike thing to suggest.'

'Well, weren't you? I mean, we've been here for three weeks and you don't seem to have a girl friend and . . . well, I just wondered.'

'Mmmmm—I was getting to the cold shower stage.'

'There, see?' But she wasn't insulted. In fact, she cuddled up closer to him.

'How about you? You weren't horny? I mean, you started the whole thing.'

Perhaps it was the dark that made confessions easier. 'I . . . I haven't had a man in two years.'

Two years. Geoff tried to imagine two years without a woman and failed. Then he wondered what had happened to her two years ago that was so traumatic that she hadn't sought out another relationship. But he knew better than to ask; Petra would only tell him when she was good and ready.

'Hey,' he said lightly, 'you've got a lot of catching up to do.'

Her tone was serious. 'Geoff, I don't think we should get involved with one another. It would be too . . . dangerous.'

'Dangerous?'

'Well, for one thing, you have to write an article on me. You might lose your perspective.'

He nibbled on her ear. 'Maybe I've lost it already.'

She shook her head. 'And I have to swim that lake. I can't let anything get between me and the swim. You see, if I . . . got . . . more involved with you . . .'

His arms tightened a bit around her. 'You can say it, Petra, it won't burn your tongue.'

Her voice was hesitant, but firmer. 'If I . . . slept with you, then I would be thinking about you and what we were doing and how it would affect me and I'd lose my ability to concentrate. I can't afford that, Geoff.'

Of course, he could see her point. He'd even known in advance what her objections would be. Aside from all the normal reasons why women were loath to get into temporary relationships, Petra had her swim to contend with. 'No,' he said heavily, 'I suppose you can't.'

'And when the swim is over ... well, you have your own life to lead. Allied Press might send you back to the Middle East or ... anywhere in the world. You wouldn't want to be tangled up with me.'

It was kind and generous of her to think about his future problems but, for some reason, it made Geoff want to grind his teeth together. 'Yeah,' he said.

Petra turned slightly to look at him although his expression was barely visible in the dark. 'That's the way you're happiest, isn't it? When you're free to do what you want?'

Geoff was confused. She was right, wasn't she? His freedom had always been his most valuable possession; his independence had given him the right to do exactly what he wanted, go where he pleased, make personal choices that weren't open to other men. He'd prided himself on his lifestyle, smugly considering himself luckier and a hell of a lot smarter than those grey-suited commuters, those buttoned-down bureaucrats, who went from office to home and back again in a mind-numbing routine. On the other hand, if his freedom was so wonderful and so valuable, why was he feeling right now as if it were a cage?

'Yeah,' he mumbled, 'I guess so.'

'So it's for the best then that we forget about tonight, isn't it?'

He felt her fear, her anxiety that he'd spend the rest of their time at the lake pursuing her as if he were a lecher in some sort of comedy routine. 'Sure,' he said. 'No problem.' And heard her sigh of gratitude.

Petra slipped out from between his loosened arms. 'Thanks for the massage,' she said.

This time he didn't try to hold her back. His arms felt like leaden, heavy weights resting in his legs. 'Any time,' he said and then cleared his throat. 'How's your headache?'

There was a smile in her voice. 'It's gone. You must be a magician.'

'Yeah.'

'Good night, then.'

'Good night.'

A magician. That was a laugh. He'd like to be a magician. With one sweep of his hand, he'd like to change everything; his crippled leg, his life, himself. But the irony was that he didn't know what he wanted to be any more. Some time during his stay in Indian Lake, Geoff had lost his focus, his goals, his perspective. The foundation of his life was shifting, altering, cracking like a house set on moving earth. Where it would settle he did not know. How it would settle, he could only guess. He only knew that some part of him refused to fall back into the old way, the old mould, the old patterns.

Look at the way he tried to make love to Petra. A month ago he would have laughed himself silly if someone had suggested that he'd even consider a physical relationship with her. She wasn't blonde, buxom and bewitching in a casual, non-threatening way. Having sex with Petra wouldn't be one of those off-hand relationships that could be eliminated with a shake of the hand or an easy goodbye. She was precisely the sort of woman that Geoff had learned to avoid at a very early stage in his adult life. She was the kind of woman that, if he got involved with her, he would have to take very, very seriously.

The thought of a relationship like that would, in the past, have sent Geoff into an overwhelming panic and a get-away whose rapidity was only exceeded by the speed of light. The fact that he didn't quite feel that way this time made him all the more confused. He hadn't changed so much that he wanted the traditional trappings of marriage, mortgage, children and nine-to-five job. He hadn't gone that crazy yet. But something was different; he just couldn't put his finger on it exactly. Geoff sighed and stood up, thankful at least that the pain in his leg had diminished to the point that he'd finally be able to sleep. Of course, an unfulfilled sexual encounter wasn't particularly conducive to a good night either, but he'd just have to grit his teeth and bear it. Perhaps that's what it all boiled down to, once again—frustration for an age-old need that plagued Geoff the way it plagued any other normal red-blooded male. Perhaps, all this confusion, this changing, this craziness, were nothing more than the symptoms of that frustration. *Perhaps*, Geoff thought tiredly as he limped his way back to bed, *I'll take a trip into Toronto and get it out of my system. Yeah, that's what I'll do.*

The police arrived at Indian Lake four days later. They came in a blue and white car with flashing, red lights, their wheels bouncing over the rutted road and sending up a dust cloud high into the trees. No one was at the cottage when they arrived except Renoir who was proving the adage that cats have nine lives. She barely acted as if she'd been the victim of a racoon or fox attack and the recipient of fifteen stitches. When the two policemen entered the cottage, she meowed at them and began to weave in and out of their legs, arching her back and sending her tail into graceful curls. She was so friendly to the police that Sunny was later to joke that Renoir had a thing for men in uniform.

The inhabitants of the cottage and Rembrandt were down at the beach, engaged in a training session—except for Sunny who was sitting in the sun, resting, her bandaged hand on her knee. She'd been doing well, to the relief of everyone. Her first day back from the hospital had been difficult. She'd not only been tired, but she'd also been determined to get back into her old routines. But it had been impossible for her to perform tasks that she'd done easily before. Cooking was hard when she couldn't use her left thumb, knitting was out of the question and sewing was awkward. It had taken her a day to admit to defeat, and they'd all breathed a sigh of relief when she'd announced the next morning that she was going on to vacation and it was up to the 'lot of them to feed their faces'. And with that, she'd grabbed a pile of magazines and marched down to the beach where she took over the best chaise-longue and took up what she called a 'career in idleness and sun-bathing'.

The rest of them had pitched in with more enthusiasm than skill, but no one criticised their results. Jennifer was assigned to breakfast detail and, although her repertory was narrow (they had scrambled eggs and toast day after day), they ate willingly. Joe and Geoff were assigned to lunches and, if their imagination was limited to ham and bologna sandwiches, no one complained. Petra was in charge of dinner since she was, after Sunny, considered the best cook. She didn't make bread or apple pies or fancy concoctions, but she knew how to keep people from starving in a way that was considered pleasant and adequate. Everyone had to help with cleaning, washing, dusting and sweeping. After three days of this, Sunny declared that she was going to go into permanent retirement.

'Over my dead body,' Joe had growled. 'You think I'm going to support you for the rest of my life?'

Sunny shrugged. 'I'm inexpensive, Joe. I don't drink, I don't buy fancy clothes, I don't spend all of your money in one place.'

'Listen to that,' Joe had implored the rest of them. 'I hand my paycheque over to her every month and don't even get an allowance.'

Sunny had given him a severe look over her glasses. 'That's a lie. You get five dollars a week.'

Geoff, Petra and Jennifer had all grinned at this, because it was common knowledge that Sunny and Joe shared a chequebook, a bank account and a petty cash system that was so casual they were always bickering over who had taken the last penny, who had a quarter for parking, where the twenty-dollar bill had gone.

Petra enjoyed Sunny and Joe's repartee; it was funny and homey and loving. She liked it so much that she often egged them on. 'Five dollars!' she said in mock-disbelief. 'Boy, Joe, I'd ask for a raise.'

'A raise?' Sunny said with horror. 'The man isn't worth more than five dollars.'

'Ah-ha,' Joe said. 'I'm not worth it, am I?'

'Not a cent more.'

'The way I pamper you and take care of you ...'

Sunny's eyebrows rose. 'Such as?'

Joe grinned. 'You want details in mixed company?'

Petra and Geoff exchanged a smile, but the innuendo had gone over Jennifer's head. 'Gee,' she said to Joe. 'I get five dollars a week allowance and I'm forty years younger than you.'

'Forty!' Joe bellowed. 'How old do you think I am, young lady?'

Jennifer giggled. 'I don't know.'

'Forty,' Joe had muttered to himself, stamping out of the cottage with Rembrandt hot on his trail. 'Forty.'

With Renoir and Sunny healing and everyone's spirits rising, the morning training sessions had taken on an idyllic air. When the police found their way down to the beach, Petra and Jennifer were doing lengths and Geoff was following them at a slower pace. He'd taken up swimming again, this time more cautiously and with better results. Joe kept an eye on him, checked his muscle tone frequently and gave him heat and leg massages afterwards. It was encouraging for Geoff to discover that if he didn't push himself too hard, that if he didn't overdo it, his body wouldn't rebel, but would instead co-operate, giving him a much-needed mobility and confidence.

Rembrandt was the first to notice the police. He scrambled out of the water in a rush, shook himself furiously, sending water all over Sunny, and then raced towards them, barking like a mad fiend. The noise attracted everyone except Petra who was on mile fifteen. She was in that other place where the outer world didn't exist and where the outside sounds didn't exist. She'd had a lot of trouble reaching that place in the past four days. It took miles of swimming before she could sink into it, letting the pain and the tiredness and the anxiety dissolve into non-existence. And, when she did finally reach that oblivion, she fell into it with an enormous relief.

Geoff, of course, was the problem. Geoff and his lazy smile and his golden hair. Geoff and the heat of his mouth and the warm stroking of his fingers. Not that he had bothered her since that night; he'd been the perfect gentleman, treating her as he had promised, as if nothing had happened. But he had awoken something in Petra that had been dormant, unaroused, unreachable by anyone else. And, in that dormancy, it had lain hidden, growing in need and desire to such a point that, when he had released it, Petra had lost control and any sense of herself as a person separate from Geoffrey Hamilton. She had wanted to merge with him so badly that night that she had almost forgotten that Geoff was a mere acquaintance and that Joe and Jennifer were sleeping just walls away and that if she actually had sex she'd stand a good chance of getting pregnant. All the strictures and restraints that she imposed upon herself had gone fleeing out of the window during those lovely moments of touching, exploring, seeking.

So she wanted to sleep with Geoffrey Hamilton. *What was wrong with that?* one part of her demanded. *Is it such a sin?* The other part, the rational, clear-headed and pragmatic Petra said, of course it isn't a *sin*, but it would be foolish and stupid and dangerous. Geoff wasn't interested in her; he was interested in sex.

Oh, he liked her; Petra knew that. But it was a fleeting, careless emotion, one that would be forgotten when he left Indian Lake and moved on to other things. He'd even admitted that he preferred freedom to any sort of entanglement.

So?—would it be so horrible to sleep with a man who, even if he isn't head over heels in love with you, would still give you some of the most pleasurable nights of your life? Well, not *horrible*, Petra said, but making love with Geoff prior to the swim would change her emotional life so much that she wouldn't be sure she could regain the equanimity, that stillness of feeling, that enabled her to endure the hours and miles that it would require to cross Lake Ontario. Look at what a small amount of ... *petting*, for heaven's sake, was doing to her concentration during training. The first twelve miles of each session had been pure, unadulterated agony.

You're crazy, Petra Morgan, to give up pleasure for agony. But Petra had thought *that* to herself so many times that she was used to discarding the idea as inconsequential. She was used to sacrificing pleasures for the purposes of swimming. She was accustomed to the rigour that demanded so much of her time that there was little left over for anything besides work and the humdrum routine of living. What other women her age considered as vital—the time to read, dance, go out with friends, watch television, follow the news, go to the movies, Petra had willingly given up for something far more vital; the chance to meet a goal few could reach, the chance to prove herself, the chance—and this was the hardest part to explain to anyone—to attain a purity of mind and spirit that was unmuddied by the dirt and chaos of life. When Petra was swimming, everything fell away; the irritations and arguments, the noise and bustle, the sadnesses and miseries. Nothing was left but the goal, the distant shore, visible before her like a single, clear, burning light.

You know, Petra, you really are crazy. But that part

of her spoke too late. The other Petra had passed mile twelve and fallen, dreamlessly, into that deep, blue and utterly silent place. She didn't hear a thing: not Rembrandt's barking; not the voices calling to her even though she was, when she turned automatically to start another lap, not more than six feet from them; not even the shrill blast of Joe's whistle. She didn't stop swimming until she did two more lengths and was, once again, approaching the beach. This time, Joe had waded out into the water and touched her on the shoulder as she approached. That sensation was so unusual it brought her immediately back into reality and she came up for air, blinking behind her goggles.

'What's the matter?' she asked. 'Was I doing something wrong?'

'No,' he said, handing her a towel. 'Come on up to the beach.'

Everyone was there when she arrived, their faces looking so anxious and drawn that Petra immediately knew that something utterly dreadful had happened. She glanced at Geoff's grim expression, the way Jennifer was biting her lip and the look of concern on Sunny's face. Then she glanced at the two policemen who were standing by the chaise-longue, looking incongruous in this setting. Their brown uniforms with the belts, holsters, guns and helmets didn't seem to fit the sun-drenched beach, the backdrop of overhanging trees, the chatter of a crow high above their heads.

'What's happened?' she asked.

But it was Sunny who spoke. 'Petra,' she said. 'The police brought a message from the hospital, the one your mother's in.' She came closer and took Petra's hand between hers, her blue eyes full of the pain she knew she was going to inflict. 'She died. Late last night.'

Six hours later, Geoff was driving Petra, in her car, into the outskirts of Toronto. She had wanted to go by herself, but Geoff and everyone else had emphatically agreed that Petra was not to make a four-hour drive alone in her condition. She had argued that she was all right, that although she was upset she was quite capable of taking care of herself, but Sunny and Joe had disagreed. Geoff had said that he'd needed to get into Toronto anyway, so the arrangements had been made despite Petra's objections.

The truth was, however, that she was quite glad to have Geoff at the wheel, coping with the rush-hour traffic and the glare of the low-lying sun on the windscreen. She had fallen asleep during the first hour of the trip and not woken until it was close to being over. It was the shock, she supposed, that had exhausted her so thoroughly. She still couldn't absorb it, the knowledge that Sheila was dead, that her mother, aged fifty-five and presumably healthy, was no longer. She remembered the last time she'd seen Sheila in the hospital. She'd been thin then, it was true, lying on her bed, her greying hair a mass against the pillow, her face pale and lined. But she hadn't been physically ill, just uninterested in food, people or activity. But Petra and the doctors had seen that sort of behaviour before. It was typical of Sheila to act that way after periods of high anxiety and paranoia. In fact, her passivity usually preceded a return to regular life as if she were gathering her energies together.

'You're up,' Geoff said, glancing sideways at her.

'I can't believe I slept that long.'

'You probably needed it.'

'I guess so.'

'What are your plans?'

'Well, the hospital has set up a funeral for the day after tomorrow.' Petra had called the administrator from a telephone booth in Mercy and agreed to all his suggestions. 'The legal aspects shouldn't be too difficult since I have power of attorney for her already. But I'll have to call a lawyer about the will, I guess.'

'Is there insurance to cover the funeral costs?'

'Some, I think.'

'Petra, I'll come with you and . . .'

'Oh, no! There's no need for you to be there.'

'But I'd like to.'

Petra glanced at him and then down at her tightly entwined hands. She didn't want pity, not Geoff's pity, not anyone's. Sheila had been her problem in life and would be her problem in death. And she was used to dealing with problems; all her life, Petra had been arranging, fixing, plotting, solving.

'It's all right,' she said.

'Petra.' Geoff's voice was firm. 'I'll come to the hospital with you and then take you to your flat. And I plan on coming to the funeral.'

'But I told you, there's no need for you to go to the trouble. I can manage just fine by myself.'

'I want to.'

'Geoff . . .'

'Don't argue.'

'But . . . why?'

Geoff deftly pulled around a lorry that was blocking two lanes of traffic. 'Why?' he echoed. 'Because you shouldn't go through this alone.'

'You're not responsible for me.' And she didn't finish the thought aloud—which was that she didn't want him thinking that just because he had kissed her, had held her in his arms, that he was automatically in charge of her.

'No, I'm not responsible for you,' he said and there was a touch of anger in his voice, 'but I'm a friend, I hope, and I'm only doing what one friend would do for another.'

Petra didn't know much about friends so she stared at him. 'Oh,' she said.

'And after the funeral, we're going to spend a couple

of days with my parents.'

'Oh! That's nice of you, but I couldn't. I have to get back to the cottage and . . .'

'I've already discussed it with Joe. He doesn't want to see you until Monday.'

'What is this?' she said, her voice rising. 'A conspiracy?'

He didn't look at her, he kept his eyes on the traffic. 'Give yourself a break,' he said. 'Give yourself a chance to recover.'

'But your parents? Why should they . . .'

'I spoke to them. They'd be delighted to have you for a few days. In fact, my mother already likes you.'

Petra blinked in confusion. 'Why?'

'Because you're bringing me with you.' He sent a sudden grin in her direction. 'My folks don't get to see me too often.'

It was all too much for Petra whose three-hour nap hadn't seemed to dissipate a feeling of exhaustion and whose overall sensation was one of numbness. It was as if she were enclosed in a glasshouse whose walls kept out loud sounds, bright lights and strong emotions. Nothing could actually get inside and grab her, not Joe's conniving behind her back, not Geoff's insistence on interfering in her affairs, not even her mother's death. Nothing could touch the cold centre of her where her heart was enclosed in ice, beating and visible but unmoved by all that had happened. Petra hadn't cried over Sheila's death, she hadn't grieved. She'd merely gone into an emotional state that resembled suspended animation.

And she simply didn't have the energy to object to the presumably kind efforts of those around her. If Joe thought he was being sympathetic by stopping her training for four days, if Geoff felt he was being generous by standing at her side at the funeral and bringing her home to his parents, Petra didn't have the force of personality to tell them differently. She didn't want Geoff's presence at the funeral; she didn't want to break her training routine, but she couldn't fight what was happening to her. Inside her glasshouse was a lethargy so pervasive that all Petra wanted to do was go to sleep again.

The administrator at the hospital, a tall, distinguished man, had had enough experience in family relations to lead Petra through the details that must be taken care of after a death with a minimum of fuss and a maximum of kindness. She was told, gently, about the unexpected and massive stroke that must have occurred in the middle of the night. 'It was probably instantaneous,' he said. 'We're sure she wasn't in pain.' She was given, in a neat package, her mother's belongings; a few dresses, a nightgown, bathrobe, slippers. She was asked if she wanted to see the body, but when she declined, that decision was accepted with understanding. She had to sign a number of forms, but the administrator didn't attempt to overwhelm her with bureaucratic regulations. Sheila's personal doctor came into the main office to offer his condolences, but this difficult occasion was kept brief and simple. In fact, she was in and out of the hospital and heading towards the suburb where she lived within an hour.

'Well,' Geoff said, 'that wasn't so bad.'

'No.' To her surprise, she hadn't minded Geoff's presence at all. He'd generally stayed in the background, only filling in the silences when they became awkward and chatting easily with the hospital staff. Petra had also been relieved to find that no one at the hospital had made any embarrassing assumption about who Geoff was. They'd accepted him as a friend of the family.

'You're going to see the lawyer tomorrow?'

'Yes.'

'And the funeral director.'

Petra nodded her head.

'You won't forget to call your insurance agent.'

'No, I won't.'

'What are you going to do tonight?'

An alarm bell went off inside of her. 'Oh, I'll be busy, and I'm ... I'm tired.'

Geoff gave her a concerned glance. 'You slept all afternoon.'

'It's been a hard day.' She glanced at the window as he pulled down a street that had a number of brick buildings with garden flats. 'Here it is,' she said. 'I live in Number 16.'

Geoff slowed the car down, pulled over to the kerb and turned to her. The elms that lined the street caught the sun in their branches and filtered its rays on to his face. One bar of illumination lay across his hair highlighting strands of gold, another emphasised the clear blue of his eyes and the worry in them. 'Petra, I don't like the idea of leaving you.'

Her hands fluttered in the air. 'I'm all right. Really, I'll be fine by myself.'

One of his hands captured hers, and the immediate sensation she had was of warmth. He was silent for a moment and then said, 'I think the doctors were sincere,' he said. 'I think she died in her sleep—if that makes it any easier.'

'Oh, I know she didn't suffer. I'm glad about that.'

'I'll call you later.'

The warmth of his hand was threatening the coldness at the centre of her, and Petra was terrified of what might happen if the iciness in her heart began to melt. 'No, you don't have to.' She pulled her hand out of his grasp. 'I might be sleeping anyway.'

His blue eyes surveyed her face. 'Tomorrow then. I'll call you tomorrow. Please, Petra, I insist.'

Reluctantly, she nodded.

'And I'll pick you up at 11:30 on Saturday for the funeral.'

'Okay.'

'And afterwards, we'll leave for my parents.'

She was too tired, to numb to care. 'All right,' she said.

Geoff leaned forwards and gently brushed his mouth against hers. 'Take care of yourself,' he whispered.

CHAPTER SEVEN

TAKE care of yourself. Had she ever done anything else?
Petra wearily unlocked the door to the flat and stepped
into its dusky interior. The windows had been closed
for a month, and the curtains were drawn tight. The air
in the living-room smelled old and stale and, in the dim
light, she could make just make out the silent forms of
furniture whose colours had long since faded into a
decor so nondescript that it merged with the greyness of
the air, the musty odour, the emptiness. Petra had tried
her best, in the past, to liven up her home with posters,
gay curtains, a colourful throw pillow, flowers, but
nothing she had done had ever survived. Sheila's
presence or the memory of her presence had dimmed
everything, so that Petra could never enter the flat
without feeling that heaviness settle over her.

And, even now, with her mother dead, the burden
was there as she walked into the rooms, wandering
from the living-room into the small kitchen and then
into her own bedroom. Dust lay on the tables and
counters, on her mother's small knick-knacks, on the
book lying beside her bed. Petra picked up the book
and glanced at it. It was a novel, but the title was
meaningless. She couldn't even remember buying it. In
some odd sort of way, Sheila's death had sheared the
past from her so that it seemed to have happened to
someone else, not the Petra who existed now, who was
idly walking through these rooms, seeing them suddenly
through a stranger's eyes, seeing herself objectively as if
a mirror were before her.

Petra Morgan, swimmer, teacher, woman, once a
daughter. She sat down on the bed and stared at the
nicked surface of her dressing-table. Once a daughter,

122

now no longer. She tasted the words on her tongue, *a daughter no longer*. They had a hard, unusual edge to them. She had been a daughter all her life. It wasn't a role she could throw off so easily, *snap*, just like that. It still clung to her so that she felt the old anxiety rise up in her. For her, being a daughter had encompassed many roles. She'd been a mother to her own mother, a protector, a breadwinner, a caretaker, a confidante, a nurturer. What would she be if she didn't play those roles? Who would she become without them?

She thought about Geoff with his offer of friendship, the hidden offer of sex. She could let him come marching into that void, couldn't she? There was nothing stopping her any more; her shameful secret didn't exist any longer. All her life, she had kept Sheila and her minimal social life at opposite poles from one another. She had spent so much effort juggling times and schedules around so that no one from her outside world would ever meet the woman who dominated her inside one. Her former lover had never even been aware that Petra actually had a mother living in the same city, much less the same flat. The stress imposed on her by that deceit had been almost unbearable.

But nothing was stopping her now. The cage around her, the cage whose steel bars had been Sheila's needs and wants and fears and dependence, had disappeared and she was free to go. She could walk into Geoff's arms and take what he was willing to give her—sex, pleasure, conversation, emotional support at a time when she could sorely use it. Oh, yes, she could use it. No matter how numb she felt, no matter how clearly her mind seemed to be working, Petra could feel her own fragility. The slightest thing would shatter it so that all her control, her poise, the tension that was holding her together in one piece would break into a thousand parts. Petra had this horrifying image of herself coming apart, the bits and pieces scattered and lost and irretrievable.

It was tempting to think about Geoff. *Take care of yourself.* He wanted to help her with that task; he wanted to help her take care of herself. She had felt that desire in him, and she knew that if she reached out, he would be there offering the solace of his body, his kindness, his generosity. How seductive that was. It would be so easy to lean on his strength; it would be so easy to fall into his willing arms, off the edge of the cliff, the narrow path of solitude and unhappiness and independence. But where would that leave her when Geoff wasn't there? When the swim was over and he had left for some remote part of the world? *A lover no longer.* She would have traded one terminated identity for one even more tentative and more unlikely to last.

Petra stood up, walked over to the curtains and pulled them open with a determined jerk of her wrist. She couldn't give up what she had spent years becoming. Even with Sheila gone, the structure of the personality that Petra had built around herself was firmly in place. She was a loner, a fighter, a coper and a survivor. And she had the swim to think about. She mustn't lose sight of what she needed to complete that swim; dedication, independence, and concentration. If she weakened and used Geoff as an emotional crutch, that weakness would be pervasive, undercutting her strengths. No, she was going to have to go it alone—as she always had, no matter what surprises came her way, no matter what fate flung in her face.

It was this attitude that enabled Petra to clean that echoing flat, to get through a sleepless night, to make the necessary phone calls the next day, and to sit in the lawyer's office and have the bombshell dropped on her without even so much as flinching.

'Well, the estate isn't much, you know,' he was saying, looking at her over his bifocals and gesturing at a sheaf of papers. The lawyer was short, rotund and balding and had been Sheila's lawyer for as long as Petra could remember.

She nodded.

'Now, as far as probate ... well, it will be simple enough. The will is quite straightforward, everything's left to you, so it's only a matter of filing the proper forms. We'll do that for you.'

Her voice was low. 'Thank you.'

'And we'll take care of the obituary if you want.'

'Yes, please.'

He cleared his throat. 'Have you notified the rest of the family?'

'There isn't anyone else.'

The lawyer shifted uncomfortably and then picked up a small manila envelope that was lying on his desk. 'Your mother gave me this years ago. She said you were to have it when she died.'

Petra glanced up at him, took it from his hand and then slowly opened it, drawing out the black and white photograph of a laughing young man. He had curly dark hair, light eyes and a happy, infectious grin. He looked like he and the cameraman had just cracked the world's funniest joke.

'Who?' she whispered and then knew.

'Your father. I told her we could track him down for her, but she wouldn't do it.' He made a tching sound with his tongue. 'I said it wasn't right. We could have got some financial support for you, but she refused.'

Petra had been under the impression that Sheila had, a long time ago, destroyed all the photographs from her courtship and marriage. For as long as she could remember, the family album, the one that held pictures of Sheila as a small girl and her dead grandparents, had also had pages that had been ripped out, their edges frayed and torn. As a result, Petra had never known what her father looked like, and she had rarely asked her mother anything about him because, the few times she had dared, Sheila had gone into rages. Now, she stared down at that seemingly carefree young man and felt the fragile egg-shell of her control waver, tremble, threaten to crack. But she took a deep breath and then slipped the photograph back into its manila sheath.

'Thank you,' she said and stood up.

The lawyer looked relieved and stood up, too. 'So,' he said, 'we'll be in touch.' Then, he cleared his throat with an awkward sound, and Petra steeled herself for what was to come. He wanted to be sympathetic, she could tell. He wanted to make her feel better about a situation that had nothing in it but distress and unhappiness. But, for some reason that she couldn't understand, acquaintances that barely knew her or her mother felt the need to comment on the occasion with trite platitudes. The insurance agent had said in a falsely hearty voice, 'Well, life does go on.' Her elderly neighbour downstairs had patted her on the shoulder and said, 'It's God's will.' Now the lawyer was about to speak his piece and Petra tried to prepare herself for it.

'She was a sick woman,' he said with a shake of his head.

'Yes.'

'Well,' he cleared his throat again and looked uncomfortable, 'sometimes these things are for the best.'

Marnie was more animated than Geoff had ever seen her. She chattered brightly, smiled at him frequently and pressed his knee under the table with her own. He couldn't decide whether it was the vast quantity of wine that she'd drunk at dinner that sparked this feverish excitement or the thrill of his presence. He'd remembered her as quiet, a bit sultry, even passive at times. Now, she was at the opposite end of the extreme. Her blue eyes glittered at him between thickened dark lashes, and she kept sweeping back her long, blonde hair with a nervous motion. And, every once in a while, she would lean far forward so that he could glimpse the creamy cleavage barely held in by her dress. Oh, she was stacked all right. That part of her had remained the same.

'. . . and I moved to a new building after the burglary. It was too scary coming home and wondering if I'd been broken into again. Of course, I had to pay an extra hundred in rent and that put a crimp into my budget. And it killed the summer holidays.'

Geoff, bored to death, gave her a winning smile. 'So what did you do?'

'Well, I *had* planned a trip out to Vancouver, I've always wanted to see the Rockies, but that was really expensive so I . . .'

Had she always been this way? Geoff looked back in the past and wondered if Marnie's conversation had always been so banal. But he couldn't ever remember talking to her. His memories were all of physical encounters; kisses in his car, lovemaking episodes in his or her bed, late-night embraces on doorsteps. Those memories made him even more restless than he was and, when Marnie had finished a full-fledged diatribe on travel agents, Geoff signalled to a waiter.

'Time to go,' he said.

'Oh . . . sure, Geoff. I'd just like to visit the ladies.'

When she was gone, Geoff paid the bill, wincing slightly at the sum and thinking that the meal hadn't been all that wonderful considering the reputation of the restaurant and the attitude of the waiter who had treated the food as if it were fit to serve royalty. But the atmosphere was what he'd been seeking, elegant and intimate, the kind of set-up where a man and a woman can sit close to one another and share a dinner without interruption or intrusion. He'd envisaged linen tablecloths, heavy silver and candles. And, having got everything he'd expected, Geoff wondered why he felt so let down.

Marnie arrived in the restaurant's foyer in full war-paint. Ever since Geoff had noticed Jennifer's over-application of make-up, he'd become aware of cosmetics. Now, he could tell that Marnie had reapplied mascara, blusher and lipstick. Her mouth gleamed at him, red and pouting. And she'd put on perfume as well. As he helped her with her raincoat, the aura of rose wafted from her neck to his nose.

Outside a light rain was falling, and Geoff had Marnie wait at the restaurant door while he limped around the block and got his car. When he picked her up, she immediately slid over to him so that their shoulders and thighs touched.

'I love the rain, don't you?' she gushed.

'As long as it keeps out of my eyes,' he said.

'You know, Geoff, I think you've changed.'

He pulled into the late night traffic. 'I have?'

'Uh-huh.'

'How?'

'Well, you're softer for one thing.'

'Softer? What does that mean?'

'I can't exactly explain it,' she said, 'but you've lost some of your edges.'

'I had edges?'

'Hard ones,' she said. 'Oh, you know, Geoff Hamilton, tough correspondent and Geoff Hamilton, dashing man about town.'

'Are you saying that my personality's changed?'

'I guess so. You're not as . . . distant.'

'I was distant with you?'

She nodded. 'You always made sure that I knew you weren't up for sale.'

Geoff glanced at her quickly and then negotiated a turn. The rain had increased in intensity and he was forced to put the screenwipers on a faster speed. 'Marnie,' he said carefully, 'I'm still not "for sale", as you put it. I'm not interested in . . .'

'Oh, I know *that*,' she said airily, 'but you're not so hard about it. You're a lot . . . nicer.'

Geoff tried to look back and call to mind the man he'd been two years ago, but it was hard to capture an image. Had he been so hard? So adamant about what he wanted? He knew that he'd been intent on getting his message across, but he'd always thought that he'd done it with subtlety and finesse. And, in addition, he'd always considered himself as generous and kind, but what Marnie seemed to be saying, in her inarticulate way, was that a cold aloofness had shown through his flirtatious charm.

'Of course,' she was saying, 'everybody changes. I've changed, too.'

'Have you?'

'I don't worry as much about things as I used to. I don't count on things. That way I'm not so disappointed when they don't turn out the way I want.'

Her voice was bright and cheerful, but Geoff couldn't help wondering how many disappointments, how many broken dreams, had brought on that attitude. Geoff knew he hadn't been the only man in Marnie's life. She was too pretty not to catch the male eye and far too sexy not to invite passes. She'd had half a dozen affairs when he'd taken her out two years before, and he could only guess at the numbers since. He'd always assumed that she'd undertaken their small liaison with the same casualness that she'd undertaken the others, but now he saw that his perceptions of her might have been wrong from the start. He'd taken her at face value, instead of wondering what went on beneath the smiles and willingness to hop into bed at a moment's notice.

He didn't speak, and Marnie leaned forward and switched on the car radio. A lilting love song filled the car and she snuggled closer to him.

'It's good to be with you again,' she said with a sigh. 'I missed you when you went to Beirut.' And then she began to hum along with the song.

It came to Geoff then that what he'd planned for the rest of the evening wasn't going to come off. He had intended to take Marnie home, accept her invitation to see her new flat, have a small drink from her liquor cabinet and then take her to bed. It had been a simple plan, easy to formulate and easy to accomplish. It hadn't taken much thinking on his part, and that's what he'd wanted—or thought he wanted—simplicity, accessibility, ease of acquisition. He'd thought of Marnie as an object that he was going to purchase with an expensive meal and then use until he was satiated with her.

But something had changed inside Geoff, something fundamental to the way he thought and acted. In the past, he'd been able to think about women as objects; as pretty faces or sexy bodies. He hadn't listened to their conversations or been interested in their personalities, but now the shield he'd protected himself with had splintered, and he could no longer maintain the arm's-length distance that he'd successfully kept in the past. Despite all his attempts to the contrary, Geoff couldn't keep himself from seeing Marnie as a 'person' instead of a woman he intended to sleep with. And, seeing her as a 'person', had a totally detrimental effect on his libido. Geoff wasn't particularly attracted to Marnie when he actually tuned into what she was saying or understood what she was like. In fact, beneath the sophistication, the cosmetic overlay, the full-blown décolletage, there was something sad and wistful about her that made him want to comfort her instead of make love to her.

He pulled up to the kerb in front of Marnie's flat and she reached down and picked up her purse.

'Coming in for a nightcap?' she asked, and her voice held a blatant hint in it.

'Marnie, I . . .'

'I remember,' she said, 'that you always liked cognac. So I got some, just for you.'

Street lights pierced the darkness in the car and picked out the brightness of her hair and her expectant eyes. Geoff leaned forward and kissed her gently on the mouth, breaking the contact when he felt her starting to respond. 'You're a sweetheart,' he said, 'but I think I'll skip it tonight.'

'Skip it?'

'Yeah, I don't think . . .'

'You mean, you don't want to come up with me?' she asked. The forlorn note in her voice was real.

Telling her the truth, Geoff saw, would have been far too cruel so he lied, tempering his decision to soften it and make it easier for her to bear. 'I'm not feeling well,' he said. 'It's my leg.'

'Oh, Geoff, I don't mind. And I've got some aspirin and . . .'

'I'm sorry,' he said. 'But I think I'd better go back to my hotel. Aspirin won't cure what I've got.'

'I wish you'd told me,' she said scoldingly, her brow creasing with concern, and he could see that she thought he'd been in pain for the whole evening. 'I thought you enjoyed dinner.'

'I did. It just started bothering me. The rain makes my leg ache.'

She was silent for a moment and then she gave a small shrug. 'Another time then.'

'Sure.'

'It was a great dinner.'

'I'm glad you enjoyed it.' Geoff turned to open his door, planning to be the gentleman and walk around the car to help her out, but Marnie stopped him.

'Your leg,' she said. 'You'd better not.'

Geoff had never blushed in his life, but now he could feel a heat in his face, and he thanked his lucky stars for the darkness. 'Right,' he said.

'Goodbye then,' she said softly and, wrapping her arms around his neck, Marnie bestowed on him a long and passionate kiss. When she was done, she touched his cheek with one finger and then slipped out of the car.

Well, so much for frustration, Geoff thought with irony as he drove off, *so much for curing what ails me.* He imagined going back to Indian Lake and being subjected to Petra's company twenty-four hours a day.

I'll be ready for cold showers and tranquillisers, he thought, *I'll be ready for* . . . And then it hit him, and he almost drove off the road in shock. In the past, he'd wanted any woman who struck his fancy, and he'd chosen long-legged blondes because they fitted a mould; he could generalise about them, he could think of them as objects, he could forget about them the moment they were out of his sight. But, for the first time in his adult life, a long-legged blonde hadn't been enough. What he wanted was not any woman, but one particular woman, and *she* didn't fit the mould at all. She was short and dark, slender and boyish, argumentative and opinionated. She was also pretty, attractive, fascinating and damned sexy. And he was falling for her . . . hell, he had fallen for her. It was even quite possible that he, Geoffrey Hamilton, playboy and philanderer, was in love with her.

Geoff tried to contemplate that thought with equanimity and discovered that he couldn't. He had to pull over to the side of the road, turn off the wipers and let the rain pound on the car's roof. He sat huddled in front of the wheel, staring out of the streaked windscreen at the headlights of oncoming cars that blurred and fragmented through the prisms of rain drops. There was no joy for him in the idea of loving Petra—she was so unlikely to reciprocate his feelings and, even if she did, was so unlikely to act upon them. There was that damned swim, her sense of independence, the way she clamped down on her emotions. Geoff knew that she was physcially attracted to him, their impassioned and ill-timed lovemaking was ample evidence of that, but he also knew that she'd hated what she'd done and how he had made her feel. Of all the women he could have fallen in love with, Petra Morgan was the worst possible choice he could have made. Logically speaking, he should have fallen for Marnie or any one of her sisters in the flesh. But love wasn't logical, it struck where it wished, a Cupid with a quiverful of capricious arrows. And Geoff, to his horror and dismay, had fallen victim. Just like that—without warning, without reason, without acceptance. Geoff didn't want to fall in love with Petra Morgan, but he had.

Goddamn it, but it seemed that he had.

'Petra! Hey, Petra! Long time, no see.'

Petra was hurrying down the length of the mall, carrying packages under her arms. She had spent the past two hours trying to find a dress that would be suitable for the funeral. She'd gone from store to store in a frenzied search for a black dress only to discover that the simple, cotton black dress didn't exist in anyone's imagination but hers—not in the summer when the racks were filled with brightly coloured halters, blouses and sundresses. She'd finally bought a dress that was a soft-grey with white-cuffed sleeves and white buttons up a demure bodice. She'd felt quite panicky until she'd found it. For some reason, it seemed extremely important that she wear the appropriate thing to her mother's funeral.

Petra came to a flying halt and blinked, staring at the man in front of her. 'Yes,' she said slowly, 'it's been a long time.'

He'd grown a moustache that was redder than his dark hair, and she thought that he'd lost some weight as well. Certainly, he looked very trim, standing there in a pair of beige chinos and a white shirt. And he was tanned as if he spent his days in the sun.

'Well, how are you?'

'Fine,' she said.

'You're looking good.'

Petra tried to smile. 'Thanks—and you? How are you?'

'Doing great. Just came back from Spain.'

'That's nice.'

There was a silence even more awkward than this

first exchange and then he said, 'I tried to phone you a couple of times,' he said.

'Did you?' she said warily.

'But I guess you were busy. Training again?'

'Yes.'

'Going to swim the lake?'

'I hope so.'

He cleared his throat. 'Hey, how about a coffee?'

The idea of spending even one more minute with him had Petra in a panic. 'No,' she said. 'I'm sorry ... I can't.'

His grin was jaunty, as if she weren't turning him down, but then Petra had forgotten how he could be. His ego didn't let him have failures. His dark eyes looked her over as if he were undressing her. 'Well, when you come out from under, give me a call, why don't you?'

What could she say except—'Okay'. Not that she ever intended to phone him or see him again, but then Petra had no experience in the handling of old and unwanted lovers. She watched him walk away, his step swaggering and confident, and she wondered bleakly what she had ever seen in him. For a second, she urgently wished that Geoff was with her, his broad shoulder above her, his hand protectively at her waist. In her mind's eye flashed a quick vision of him from a week before at the lake. He'd been talking to Joe on the porch, lying down on the couch, wearing only a pair of shorts, his hands tucked underneath his head. His chest, flat and wide, was sprinkled with golden hairs, there were tufts of gold in his armpits. Down her glance had gone; down the breadth of his ribs to the ridged abdomen, down to legs that were lean and muscular and crossed at the ankle. And then she had turned away, feeling the warmth rise within her, that unwanted warmth.

It came to Petra then that Geoff was the first man that she had ever truly wanted. In fact, she hadn't known about desire before meeting him. Any other emotion that she'd felt with anyone else had been a sham, a facsimile of the real thing. She'd grown up without a man in the family, and she'd spent too isolated a childhood and adolescence to know what men were like. It wasn't any surprise that she would have willingly gone to bed with the first man who made a serious effort to sleep with her. She'd been curious; she'd wanted the experience, but she hadn't really wanted *him*. He'd only been an object, someone she was manipulating to satisfy needs that had nothing really to do with sex.

But her feelings about Geoff were different. Petra couldn't exactly sort them out. She liked him, wanted him, enjoyed him, was intrigued by him—a whole mix of emotions that tangled in her mind like a skein of yarn. No strand had an end or a beginning, each ran into the other in a confusing way. She couldn't separate her desire to sleep with him from her desire to talk to him from her desire to be with him. And, also tangled among these golden threads were the dark ones; her own fears, her need for independence, her distrust of people in general and men in particular, her knowledge that once the swim was over Geoff would be gone— happily and willingly.

Petra shook her head and gathered her packages closer to her, forcing thoughts of Geoff away. She still had so much to do before the funeral. There were Sheila's clothes that had to be packed and given away to some charitable organisation; there were her books, her papers, her crocheting, and her knick-knacks. Petra only wanted to save a few things; the pieces of jewellery that were worth something, a fancy perfume bottle that Sheila had owned since she was a teenager, the file of recipes that had been so exhaustively written out and indexed. It had saddened her immensely to discover that in fifty-five years of life, Sheila had left so little that was of any lasting importance.

Petra left the mall and put her packages into the boot of her car. Her last stop before going home was a visit to the minister of a nearby church. He had asked her to stop by and talk to him a bit about her mother so that he could give a fitting funeral benediction. Like all the professionals that Petra had had to consult in the past day, the lawyer and the insurance agent, he barely knew Sheila. In her last years, she'd grown too paranoid to step out of the house and go to church. He'd visited her a couple of times, but as she spent more and more of every year in the hospital, even those visits had tapered off to nothing. Petra sighed as she opened her car and slipped into the front seat. She didn't know what she could tell the minister about a woman whose grasp of reality was so weak that, half the time, she hadn't even been able to recognise her own daughter.

It didn't quite rain on the morning of the funeral, but the sky was a dark grey and a mist fell now and again. The mourners didn't wear raincoats but were carrying umbrellas and, as Geoff looked around him, all he could see from his height was a small sea of bobbing unbrellas. Only Petra stood bare-headed in the mist, her hair dampening and curling, and he ached to touch her, to comfort her, to ease her somehow, but her body language was so emphatically negative that Geoff knew better. From the way she was standing with her hands clenched at her sides, it was obvious that she wanted to be alone. The other mourners, the doctor from the hospital, a couple of nurses, and several neighbours, had also sensed her need for isolation. They had murmured condolences to her and then stepped away. Glancing at her now, Geoff saw the tension in her shoulders and the rigid hold of her head. He wondered what was going on inside her, what battles were being fought, what maelstrom of emotions was building to a pitch so high that she had to hold herself tight enough so that it wouldn't break loose. He wondered if she had cried for her mother, but he suspected that she hadn't. He thought he knew Petra well enough to guess that it would be near impossible for her to find a release for her grief. She was probably frantic to get back to the lake so she could throw herself into training once again. That was the Petra Morgan solution to problems that were too big to go away.

Both Geoff and Joe had understood this and had felt that it was unhealthy. When Geoff had suggested to Joe that he take Petra to his parents' home for a few days after the funeral, the trainer had expelled a breath of relief.

'She's going to need some winding down,' he'd said, 'or she'll burn herself out in the water.'

'She'll be forced to rest,' Geoff had reassured him. 'My father's retired and my mother's idea of a day's work is a short trip into town to get some more reading matter. They're easy-going people.'

'Sounds good,' Joe had replied. 'Just let Petra know she's forbidden to come back for a few days. I don't want to see her, no matter how much she hassles you. Got it?'

'Got it.'

What Geoff hadn't said at the time was that he also hoped that his family would do something else for Petra. He sensed, rather than knew, that there was a part of Petra that was raw and painful and afraid. He didn't know all the reasons why this was so, but even before the death of her mother, he'd been sensitive enough to catch the edges of a sadness that lay beneath the strong personality and the defiant independence. What he wanted was for the warmth and love and closeness of his family to envelop Petra, to shield her from her grief, her cares, her anxieties. He knew how his father would welcome her and how his mother would fuss over her. They'd pamper her and then some, and Geoff knew how much Petra's life had lacked in pampering. She didn't talk very much about her childhood, but Sunny had filled him in on the details.

'She's had a hard time of it,' Sunny had said one afternoon when they were sitting alone on the small spot of grass outside the cottage, sharing a rectangle of sun. He's asked her about Petra's background and then, when she'd given him a look of suspicion, he'd assured her that he wouldn't use it in an article.

'In what way?'

'Her childhood was bad, really bad. Her father deserted the family when she was small, and her mother's crazy.'

'Crazy?' Geoff tried to understand what Sunny was saying. 'You mean, really crazy?'

'She spends most of her time in that mental institution north of Toronto.'

'What's wrong with her?'

Sunny gave an unhappy sigh. 'I don't know exactly. Schizophrenia perhaps.'

Geoff didn't know very much about schizophrenia, but he did know enough about mental illness to guess how devastating it must have been for Petra to live with a mother who was certifiably insane. 'I see,' he said slowly.

Sunny took a pin out of her hair, tucked some strands back into her bun and then stuck the pin back in again as if she would have liked to jab something else rather than her own head. 'And Petra's had to support the two of them, take care of her mother and organise her own life since she was a teenager. I've always been amazed and impressed that she made it through college and got herself a decent job. There's plenty of people out there who would have used a history like that to end up on welfare.'

Geoff was silent for a while and then he said, 'I suppose that explains the swimming, too.'

'Sure,' said Sunny. 'Joe says it's the only thing she's got that counts for anything, and it's the only outlet she's got to escape from her life. If you wanted to know what makes Petra swim, there you've got it in a nutshell.'

'And she doesn't want anyone to feel sorry for her.'

'God, no! Petra doesn't indulge in self-pity either, at least, not that I've noticed.' Sunny looked at Geoff through her dark glasses. 'She's an impressive woman.'

'Yes.'

'But very vulnerable to certain things.'

'Such as?'

'Such as ... well, to put it bluntly, men.'

Geoff returned her look. 'Meaning what?'

'Meaning,' said Sunny, 'that I'm not blind to what's going on.'

It was too much to expect that Sunny who had a voracious interest in everything that went on around her would have missed the over-polite interchanges between Petra and himself. Ever since the night they'd met on the porch, they'd been cautious with one another, deferring to each other, passing the salt with pleases and thank-yous and carefully avoiding any physical contact.

Geoff gave her a non-repentant grin. 'Sunny, you've got an eye like a hawk.'

She waved a finger at him. 'If you hurt that girl,' she said, 'you'll be sorry.'

'It's okay,' he said ruefully, 'she doesn't want me.'

'Ah. Well, isn't that smart of her?'

'That's not very complimentary.'

'Tell me something, Geoff. Are you interested in a lifetime commitment to one woman?'

'No.'

'That's what I figured,' she said smugly, sitting back in her chair and putting her face to the sun. 'That's just what I figured.'

Of course, Geoff hadn't known then that he loved Petra. He'd only thought of her as a diversion, a small and sexy diversion. But now it was different. His heart

went out to her, standing by the graveside of her
mother, a slender, tiny figure, dressed in grey, her head
bent, her back so stiff and rigid. He wanted to fold her
into his arms and pour into her, if this sort of osmosis
was possible, all the healing force of his love. But he
couldn't. Like all the others around him, he was forced
to stand away from her, knowing that somewhere
hidden in that silent figure, a woman was crying and
hurt and in pain.

The minister finished his benediction and a cloth was
laid over the coffin. Slowly, those who had attended the
ceremony paid their respects to Petra and then left. It
wasn't until everyone was gone that Geoff finally
approached her. She had not moved from where she
had been during the funeral, but she no longer seemed
to know what was going on around her. And, she was
so engrossed in her inner thoughts that she never heard
the soft sound of his footsteps or even noticed when he
touched her.

'Petra?' Below his fingers, he could feel the damp
fabric of her dress and, below that, the slender bones of
her shoulder. The mist had started again, its drops so
fine that it appeared as a fog, shrouding them in its
greyness.

She turned to face him, and he saw that her eyes,
dark and huge in the paleness of her face, were
absolutely dry. 'Yes?' she asked, and there was no
recognition of him in her glance. It was if she had never
seen him before, as if he were a total stranger.

Geoff felt the pain of it pierce him in some visceral,
vulnerable place, but he never flinched. He merely said
as softly and as gently as he could, 'Come. It's time to
go.'

CHAPTER EIGHT

THERE wasn't a bit of water near the home of Geoff's parents; not a pond, not a lake, not a stream, not a river. Not one place that Petra could swim in if she had wanted to, which was why Geoff had chosen it as a retreat of sorts in the first place. The house itself was large and comfortable, set on an acre of land in an old neighbourhood where the elms had grown to huge heights, the hedges were lush and thick, the pavements old and cracked from the thousands of small feet that had bicycled on them, run on them and played hopscotch on them. Even though the Hamilton boys were all grown, it was still a neighbourhood of children. The peace of the summer days was periodically broken by laughter, screams and high-pitched voices yelling at one another. It was the kind of neighbourhood where children grew up healthy and straight. It was the kind of neighbourhood that Petra had dreamed about as a little girl, but had never experienced.

On her first morning there, Petra dug her sneakers out of her suitcase, put on a pair of shorts and a T-shirt and went jogging. Her slender figure and dark hair could be glimpsed through the trees from the back patio where Geoff and his parents were having breakfast. The patio had an old glass-topped table, plastic chairs that had seen better days and a couple of fly swatters to kill the insects that liked to share Hamilton meals and barbecues. As long as Geoff could remember, his family had eaten out of doors during the summer.

'She's an interesting girl,' Geoff's mother, Marion, remarked as she poured herself a cup of coffee. She was a small woman with salt-and-pepper hair and quick

141

bird-like motions, still almost as pretty as the girl she had once been. 'Isn't she, dear?'

'Dear' was Geoff's father, Matthew, who usually spent his mornings buried in the *Globe and Mail* and *The Toronto Star*. He'd been a stockbroker once, but upon retirement, he'd announced that he'd preferred politics to investments and now spent hours reading about politicians, elections and scandals. Other than that, he was a loving husband, a kind and generous father to his four sons and an adoring grandfather to three diminutive granddaughters.

'Yes,' he said absent-mindedly. Geoff's parents often held a three-way conversation between themselves and the newspaper. When they did this, all that could be seen of Matthew was the top of his head with its thinning grey hair. When he lowered the paper, the rest of him would come in view—a face with a strong jaw like Geoff's and mild blue eyes beneath rather fierce-looking eyebrows.

'Sad though,' Marion went on. 'Very sad. Don't you think so, dear?'

'Very,' Matthew agreed.

It would have been hard not to come to that conclusion. Petra and Geoff had arrived after dinner the night before and, no matter how hard Petra had tried to respond to the Hamiltons' warm welcomes, her wan smiles and attempts at enthusiasm had been totally unconvincing. At nine-thirty, she'd said that she had a headache and had gone to bed. Geoff had to give his parents high marks for their restraint after that. They'd neither grilled him about her or made any comments although, knowing his mother as he did, Geoff wasn't surprised that her curiosity had finally surfaced this morning.

'My heart just went out to her, Geoff. I've never seen anyone with such . . . haunted eyes. She must have been close to her mother.'

'I don't know,' Geoff said, buttering a piece of toast.

'Her mother was sick, mentally ill. She'd spent most of the last few years in an institution.' When he'd phoned his parents from Mercy, Geoff had only offered them the bare bones of the situation. They knew that Petra was a marathon swimmer, they knew that Geoff was covering her swim, and they knew that her mother had died. Other than that, he'd left them in the dark. He knew that just the fact that he was bringing a woman home with him would cause enough of a stir.

Marion's face took on a look of shock. 'Oh, Geoff,' she said. 'I had no idea. Matthew, did you hear that?'

Geoff's father put down his newspaper. 'Yes,' he said, 'I did.'

Marion intervened. 'There's no father, is there, Geoff?'

'No. He disappeared when she was young. Petra had a hard childhood, there wasn't much money and not a lot of emotional support either.'

Marion liked to think of herself as an amateur psychologist. 'Do you suppose that has something to do with her swimming? I mean it's a rare person who decides to tackle a lake.'

'I think so,' Geoff said. 'It's an outlet for her, it's a way she can prove her own worth. It's probably even more than that. She's a complex person.'

'Well,' said Marion, 'that will make for an interesting article.'

Geoff shook his head. 'I don't plan on writing about her past.'

Marion blinked with surprise. 'No? I would have thought that would be the best part.'

And then, with the sort of acuity that had characterised his days at the Toronto Stock Exchange, Matthew bypassed the idea that Geoff's compassion towards Petra had anything to do with his role as journalist and said, 'You're pretty serious about this girl, aren't you?'

Marion gave her husband a startled glance. 'I don't think . . .' she began.

'I'm in love with her,' Geoff said.

There was a long silence around the patio table as Geoff applied marmalade to his buttered toast and took a large bite. Both his parents watched this process with utter fascination as if they'd never seen him eat before.

Finally, Marion said, 'Geoff, I don't know what to say. You've just taken my breath away.'

Matthew said, 'Perhaps, congratulations are in order.'

Geoff shook his head. 'Not exactly.'

But Marion hadn't heard this. The ramifications of his announcement were just starting to make themselves clear, and her head had got quite wrapped up in such details as engagements, bridal showers and weddings. 'You know,' she said, a bit breathlessly, 'you're the last of my boys to get married. Second oldest, but the last to settle down. Tom's got the two little girls already, and David's got one daughter and as for Alex . . . well, I mean they haven't officially told me yet, but I'm sure Fiona is pregnant. It would be nice if it were a boy, but your father and I don't ask for anything except a healthy baby.' She took a deep breath. 'And now you . . . I can hardly believe it. I never thought I'd see the day that . . .'

'Mom?'

His voice stopped her and the sad smile on his face. 'What?'

'I'm not getting married.'

'Oh.' Marion glanced at Matthew for help.

'You're living with her?' Matthew asked.

'No, I'm not. I'd like to be, but I'm not.'

'Oh, Geoff,' said Marion with a sigh, 'I wish I could understand these modern relationships. It isn't that I disapprove, it's just that I can never quite figure out what's going on.'

'Well, in this case, you don't have to worry, because

nothing's going on at all. In fact, I'm afraid that the young lady in question doesn't reciprocate my feelings.'

There was another silence as Geoff poured himself another coffee, added a bit of milk and then a dollop of sugar. This time his parents were busy looking elsewhere. Marion was giving Matthew a helpless look while he was rummaging through his paper as if trying to find the answers to the most profound questions in the universe.

'Well,' Marion said. 'What can we do to help?'

Geoff gave his mother a grin. 'I thought it might be nice if she saw what a great family I have, what a friendly bunch we are. She might think better of me then.'

'Geoff.' Marion put her hand on his. 'How can she not think well of you? You're the best-looking of all my boys, quite possibly the smartest and without a doubt the most dashing. You've broken more hearts than all the others combined.'

'You know something, Mom? I always feel better when I know that you're on my cheering squad. Of course, it could be that you're prejudiced.'

Marion sat back. 'Never,' she said haughtily. 'Right, dear?'

But Matthew was once again immersed in his paper. He had, after all, lived through the raising of four boys and been the observer of at least a dozen of their love affairs. He knew better than to interfere, comment or otherwise get himself unduly concerned about matters he couldn't influence even if he'd wanted to. 'Right,' he said. 'Anything you say.'

Petra felt as if she were surrounded by versions of Geoff. There was the shorter, squarer version who was Tom, the taller, lankier version who was David and the pudgier one who was Alex. All the brothers had the same wavy, golden hair, blue eyes, tanned complexions and square chins. It was uncanny to look around the dinner table and see four men who looked as if they'd all been cut from the same cookie-cutter.

Of course, they weren't, personality-wise, the same at all. She'd already learned during the course of the evening that Tom was serious, David was an extrovert and Alex was shy. And they had all arrived with their wives, none of whom looked alike and, if they had any, their children. The dining-room in the Hamilton home was a mad-house. Tom's daughter Melissa, three years old and already a hellraiser, refused to sit in her high-chair and would have thrown a temper tantrum if Grandpa hadn't intervened and sat her on his lap. Her sister Amanda was happily banging a spoon on the tray of her high-chair while David's daughter Penelope was letting her presence in the playpen be known by alternating loud noises with experimental whimpers. All the children were clearly Hamiltons. Even the smallest had those tell-tale golden curls.

Above the noise supplied by the children, the adults in the family were carrying on a raucous conversation over the merits and failures of the Conservative government. From what Petra could gather, the family was intensely split over party loyalties and vehement words were being exchanged over Liberal policy versus that of the New Democratic Party concerning recent laws on trade unions, the minimum wage and tax hikes. It was all very voluble and very emphatic with Matthew pounding his fist on the table and Tom getting slightly red in the face. But, just at the moment when the controversy hit its most acrimonious point, and Petra was sure a family feud would ensue, Alex's wife Fiona said something amusing and the conversation fell into much laughter. Petra had never really seen anything quite like it. Mealtimes when she had been growing up had been either silent or lonely.

The roast beef was cleared away along with the jellied salad that Tom's wife Wendy had brought, the mashed potatoes, the cole slaw and the Harvard beetroot. 'Matthew adores beetroot,' Marion had confided to Petra when she'd helped with dinner. 'No one else will touch them. But you know how it is, you have to pamper a man a little or he gets grumbly.' In fact, Petra didn't know how it was, she had no idea how one was supposed to treat a husband, but Marion seemed to be doing such a good job of it, that she filed the information away in that place in her head that wondered about men and relationships.

Once the main courses were put away, the dessert arrived to an enormous fanfare. Geoff gave an admiring whistle, Melissa drummed on the table, Matthew gave a loud hurrah and David's wife Jeannie blushed because the two apple pies, their tops baked to a golden brown, a savoury steam rising from the cuts in the crust, were hers.

'Cut them up fair and square, Mom,' said Alex. 'No playing favourites.'

'Have I ever cheated you?' Marion said tartly.

'A million times,' he replied cheerfully. 'I'll never forget that lemon meringue pie.'

'Me either,' said David. 'That was the best lemon meringue pie I've ever had.'

'That,' Alex said, 'was because you got the biggest piece. Mom cut you the biggest piece and we all had a fit.'

'No, it was Geoff.'

Geoff gave them an innocent look. 'Me?'

Tom stepped in. 'You sneaked a piece. Remember?'

'For heaven's sake,' Marion exclaimed. 'I don't even know what pie you're talking about. Do you know, dear?'

Matthew, who was bouncing Melissa on his knee, shook his head. 'Nope.'

Geoff had leaned back in his chair and was idly studying the ceiling. 'One you baked in . . . let's see, was it 1969?'

'1971,' said Tom.

''72,' said David. 'I was in grade 10.'

Marion put down the knife she'd been wielding on

one of the pies. 'If you boys don't quit arguing now, none of you will get any of this.'

Geoff immediately straightened up while his brothers either saluted or tried to look appropriately terrified. Marion threw Petra a can-you-believe-this look and then shook her head in disgust. Petra smiled back at her and, for a second, had a vivid vision of what it must have been like for Marion and Matthew to bring up four rambunctious, loud and noisy boys. She imagined a kitchen with boys sitting on the edges of chairs, digging through the refrigerator, applying peanut butter to bread and, just generally, making a nuisance of themselves. She imagined a dinner table where grubby hands were prevalent, the conversation was about hockey or baseball and milk was drunk in huge quantities. She didn't exactly envisage the Hamilton life as idyllic as a television sitcom; she knew it must have had its bad spots and rough patches, but she did capture the emotional context of love, appreciation and loyalty.

The pie was distributed evenly, coffee was served and the post-dinner conversation was much quieter with Melissa's mouth full of pie and the two other babies soothed with bottles. It was at that time that the conversation ambled gently and then, just as if the Hamiltons had given her a chance to get acclimatised and now thought she was ready for their attention, the whole family focussed on Petra and her swim.

She had to describe her training sessions, explain how the swim was organised, how the weather would affect what she did, the sort of bathing suit she'd wear, how she would eat, drink and protect her skin against the water.

'Aren't you afraid?' Wendy asked. 'I mean, I'd be terrified.'

Petra thought about that for a moment. 'Terrified of what?' she finally asked.

'Fish,' Tom said, giving his wife a humorous glance. 'She'd be afraid a trout would get her.'

'Actually,' said Petra, 'there once was a swimmer that had his trunks torn off by a huge salmon. They could see it in the radar.'

'There,' said Wendy triumphantly to Tom, 'you see? I'm not so crazy after all.'

'Well,' said Marion, 'I, for one, would be terrified of drowning. How deep is Lake Ontario? Miles to the bottom?'

Geoff reached across the table and patted her hand. 'Mom, you're the world's lousiest swimmer.'

'Still,' she said, 'what if even a good swimmer gets tired? I'm sure that some of those marathon swimmers didn't make it.' And she looked to Petra for help.

'There was a guy who tried to cross in the mid-seventies,' Petra said. 'He had one boat with him and a friend who was pacing him occasionally. A wind came up and they got separated from the boat. The friend wanted to stay in one place, but the swimmer insisted on going ahead. Eventually the two of them separated as well. The boat came back and managed to pick up the friend, but they never found the swimmer.' There were grimaces around the table. 'But I don't worry about that. Swimmers are better protected now. I'll have four boats with me, and my trainer wouldn't let me stay in the water if it gets too rough or cold.'

'Still,' said David, 'I can understand why that swimmer didn't want to give up. It must be hard as hell to give up in the middle.'

Petra gave him a shy smile. 'That's the swimmer's nightmare.'

'I'll never forget when that little girl swam the lake back in the fifties,' Marion said. 'Bell, that was her name. Marilyn Bell. My father was in the hospital then after his accident with a broken back and two broken legs. He was terribly depressed, and even the doctors worried that he'd give up. But one night he was listening to the reports of her swim on the radio, and he turned to my mother and me and said, "If that little girl can do it, if she can have the courage to swim that huge lake, well, by God, I'll have the courage to get through this."' Marion leaned toward Petra. 'I think it's wonderful what you're doing. You're an inspiration to those of us who can only dream.'

Petra was too embarrassed by that to do anything but smile and look down at the table, but before she did, she caught a glimpse of Geoff's face. He had, during the course of her stay, treated her with a friendly casualness. He hadn't touched her in any proprietary way; he hadn't acted towards her as if she were anything more than an acquaintance. And his family had taken the hint. If they were wondering if Geoff and Petra were more to one another than friends, they didn't show it. So dinner had been relaxed, and Petra had seen Geoff smiling at her occasionally and, when she spoke, bestowing on her the same interest that the rest of the Hamiltons had given her. But after his mother's words, he wore an odd expression. Petra couldn't read it, she couldn't tell what he was thinking. His face had become serious and a slight frown wrinkled his forehead. And his eyes rested on her with a look that mixed bewilderment, reflection and something else that she couldn't identify at all.

Geoff only realised that Petra had disappeared after Tom and Wendy had finally got their two children in hand and made farewells that seemed to go on for half an hour. There had been such a bustle and confusion in the foyer of grown-ups and children and car beds and nappy bags that she had slipped away without anyone noticing that she was gone. Geoff quickly said goodbye to his two remaining brothers and their wives and then went upstairs. But when he reached her bedroom and knocked on the door, there was no answer. And, on opening the door, he discovered that it was empty. Her suitcase sat neatly on the chair, the shorts and T-shirt she'd worn earlier in the day were folded neatly in the bed. He let out his breath with relief, suddenly realising how frightened he'd been. He'd actually thought she might pack up her belongings and depart, and his fear had come from knowing that she was here against her will, that he and Joe had forced her into coming.

'Geoff? Is anything the matter?' Marion was standing in the hall, watching him.

'I thought Petra might be in here.'

'Perhaps she went for a walk.' Marion gave a small laugh. 'Perhaps she needed some peace. We Hamiltons can be pretty overwhelming sometimes.'

'I thought she enjoyed dinner.'

'I think she did, but she's unhappy, Geoff. There's so much sadness in her. It might have been asking an awful lot to have her put up with us after her mother's death.'

'I don't know. I can never tell what Petra's thinking.'

'She's a challenge to you, isn't she?'

'Very,' he said drily.

'That's what you need, you know, a challenge. You've never been one to like what comes easily.'

'I thought I did,' he said.

They might have been talking in a sort of shorthand, but Marion knew precisely what Geoff was saying. The names of too many women had been spoken in the past fifteen years; hints of too many casual affairs had been dropped in the parental lap.

'I know,' she said gently, 'but it seems that you've changed.'

Geoff opened the back door of the house and stepped out into the night. There was a full moon, casting its ivory illumination over the garden so that the huge elms threw deep shadows and the high hedge seemed to be a sculpture in modulated shades of grey. He traversed the

patio, peering into the yard and calling softly, 'Petra?'
There was no voice answering him back, only the
sounds of crickets and the occasional flash of a
lightning bug. Every now and again, a slight breeze
swayed the branches of the trees, sending the leaves into
a hectic rustling, but then it would die off and
everything would be still until the crickets started up
again.

It was a beautiful night. Stars sprinkled the black
dome of the sky, the moon was a giant, unblinking eye.
The smell of summer night was prevalent, a mixture of
honeysuckle, lilac and warm earth. Geoff stepped on to
the grass and felt its softness yield beneath his feet. He
had kicked off his sandals during dinner and could feel
the blades tickling his toes. With his awkward limp, he
walked deeper into the garden, but still could see
nothing. Perhaps she had decided to take a walk around
the block, he thought and began to turn in the direction
of the front of the house when he caught a glimpse of
white near the largest of the elms, the tree that the
Hamilton boys had once built a rickety house in and
hung a tyre swing from. He remembered that Petra was
wearing the light grey dress that she'd bought for the
funeral. It was pale enough to turn to white under the
moon's strong light.

'Petra?'

No answer.

Geoff walked towards that tiny smudge of white,
passing by the badminton net, his mother's small herb
garden, the stump of a huge tree that had died and been
cut down. He brushed aside the overhanging branch of
a dogwood and walked until that tiny smudge of white
grew large enough to reveal the form of a woman sitting
with her back to the tree, her knees drawn up to her
chin, her arms wrapped tightly around her legs. Her
hair was dark enough to meld in with the surrounding
blackness, but her face was a tiny, shadowed oval.

Geoff knelt down beside her. 'Petra? Are you okay?'

But she still didn't answer so he reached out and, with his fingers bent, gently touched her cheek with his knuckles. He felt the dampness immediately, felt the fulness of a tear rolling down her skin. It fell on to his finger and trembled there before dropping off on to the grass.

'Oh, Petra,' he said, groaning, 'for God's sake.' And he forgot the injunction she'd placed on him, the restraint against any physical contact, and he pulled her into his arms, the sadness in her communicated to him by the way she drew in a shaky breath, curled into him and pressed her eyes against his shoulder. He put his hand on the back of her neck, rested his cheek against the springiness of her hair and held her as tight as he could while she cried. He held her while she shook and sobbed. He held her while the crisp fabric of his shirt went limp under the onslaught of her tears. He held her until she finally stopped and simply rested, her breathing uneven and erratic.

'I'm sorry,' she finally said, her voice muffled against his shoulder.

'For what?'

'For . . . for you having to witness this.'

'Petra, there's no shame in crying.'

'It's just self-pity.'

His arms tightened around her. 'Maybe you have a right to feel sorry for yourself. After all, your mother has just died. Did you think you were going to walk away from the funeral as if it hadn't happened?'

'But . . . it's not just that.'

'No?'

She sat up a bit so that Geoff's arms formed a loose circle around her. 'It's a whole mix of things,' she said despairingly. 'Of horrible things.'

'Like what?'

'Like . . . well, that I'm sad over her death. I loved her . . . I really did. She was my mother, but . . . well, part of me is so *angry* at her.' Her voice quavered and then she rushed on as if to keep one step ahead of the tears. 'I found out from the lawyer that she'd refused to get in contact with my father, that she could have done it but didn't want to.'

'But didn't your father leave when you were small?'

'Yes, but that doesn't mean I didn't want to see him or know what he was like, but she lied to me about him. She said that he'd disappeared, that no one knew where he was, that he didn't ever want to see us again. I mean, I suppose it's partially the truth, I don't suppose he left because he loved her and if he'd really cared about me, he would have tried to make contact. But the thing is that we could have found him, the lawyer wanted to do it for us.'

Geoff could understand why Petra was angry, but he could also imagine what her mother must have felt. 'Maybe she couldn't face seeing him again.'

Petra heaved a shaky sigh. 'I know. I can understand it, but part of me is so ... angry. And then ...' the tears were starting again, Geoff could sense their rising in the timbre of her voice, '... and then, although I cared for her ... really cared for her ... well, I'm just ... relieved that she's gone.'

The last was said with a despairing wail, and Geoff took Petra's face between his hands. 'It's okay,' he murmured, 'it's okay.'

'I mean, underneath I'm *happy* that she's dead. All those years of taking care of her, of having to watch her and worry about her. Geoff, you don't know the times that I've found her wandering around the streets half-dressed or I've been called up by a shop where she'd tried to buy something without money or had the police ringing the door asking me to identify her because they'd found her huddled in an alley somewhere. She was crazy, Geoff, and I'm ... I'm glad she's dead.'

He knew better than to say anything. He merely brushed away the tears from her upturned face with his thumbs, keeping her face between his hands, and she grasped his wrists, desperately, as if she were drowning and he were her lifeline.

'I hated her sometimes. When I was a kid, I wanted to believe that she wasn't my mother. I used to have this fantasy where there would be a knock on the door and I would open it and a beautiful woman would be standing there—my real mother, coming to find me after having been forced to put me up for adoption. I didn't think too much about *why* she'd put me up for adoption.' Petra sniffed and gave a small, shaky laugh. 'I just wanted her to be there and take me away into some dream life where I had a mother and a father who weren't crazy, where I could have birthday parties and friends overnight and help with my homework and ... it was dumb, I know, but that's the way I was. And I felt guilty about it, because I wasn't being loyal. I wasn't loving my own mother enough.' She paused and then went on. 'And then I grew up and understood that even having two normal parents isn't the answer to everything. But it still hurts. It hurts like it did tonight at dinner. I almost hated you and your family, Geoff, because you're all so happy, because you and your brothers had all the important things without even trying or asking, because you're all so damned healthy and well-adjusted and normal.'

A glimmer of understanding came to Geoff. 'You're normal, too.'

'No, I'm not. I'm not like most people. How many normal people try to swim a thirty-two-mile lake?'

'People who have goals, who have a need to prove themselves.'

Between his hands, Petra's head moved vehemently from side to side. 'No, I'm not just one of those,' she said. 'You once told me that people who do these sorts of things are trying to be in control, and you were right. You see, I was afraid, terrified that if I didn't control something in my life, if I didn't focus on one thing to the exclusion of everything else, I'd go crazy. Like my mother. Her mind wandered, Geoff, she

couldn't remember anything, she couldn't stick to
anything. She'd start vacuuming the flat, forget about it
and rearrange her recipes. Then she'd forget about
that and iron a skirt. And then forget about that. I'd
come home and find the flat in a mess because she'd
started half a dozen things and given up and was
watching television. When I'd ask her what she'd done,
she'd be bewildered and upset because she couldn't
remember. I . . . I didn't want to be like that.'

'Oh, Petra,' he said, his heart going out to her.
'You're not like that at all. You're one of the sanest
people I know.'

She tugged on his wrists, pulling his hands down
from her face so that they rested, empty and helpless, in
the darkness. 'But you don't know what goes on in my
head. I've been so afraid. I could never get close to
anyone or confide in anyone or trust anyone. I've never
understood before why I was like that, but I've come to
realise that I'm afraid someone will get close enough to
find out that I'm just like my mother. I've been
terrified, Geoff, absolutely petrified that someone was
going to discover that everything I do is just an act, that
underneath I'm crazy, insane, a nut that should be
committed to a looney bin.' She gave a harsh, bitter
laugh. 'So you see why I came out here. I've been
feeling very sorry for myself.'

It was all clicking in place, all the parts of Petra that
hadn't made any sense to Geoff were now revealed and
fitting together so he could understand who she was, a
woman whose past existed so strongly in the present
that, although she was now an adult, she couldn't
forget the fears and angers of childhood and couldn't
separate herself from the mother who had harmed her.
And it had taken a death, a funeral, a revelaton of a
lawyer to bring all those hidden emotions up to the
surface where, in a volcanic fashion, they had exploded
within her, breaking her down, forcing her to cry. Geoff
remembered that tense, rigid figure at the graveside

with the tortured, dry eyes, and he knew how important it was that her grief and anger was expressed instead of held in where it would eat away at her, corrode her very soul. *Thank God*, he thought, *that she's finally been able to cry.*

She went on, 'I'm afraid I haven't been a very good guest.'

Gently. 'No one expected anything of you.'

'I meant to tell you—your parents are very nice and so are your brothers and their families.'

'I'm glad you like them.'

'And ... I apologise for giving you such a hard time about bringing me here. I didn't want to come, I wanted to get back into the lake and swim until I dropped.'

'That's what Joe and I figured.'

She was silent for a moment and then said, 'So now there's only the lake left.'

But this was said in such a forlorn tone that Geoff said, 'But your life isn't going to end with that swim.'

'I know, but I can't think any further ahead. The swim is just looming ahead of me. I put up a brave front for your family, but I'm afraid of it. Afraid of how much it will hurt, of how cold it will be, of the way I might fail. I want to do it, but I'm afraid.'

'It's okay to be afraid.'

Petra smiled at him, and he could just make out the upturn of her mouth in the moonlight. 'You're very nice to me, Geoff. I can be afraid, I can feel sorry for myself, I can cry buckets on your shoulder.' The little laugh she gave was low, rueful and wondering. 'How come you're so nice to me?'

There are moments in life which arrive without warning, moments where a certain phrase, an assortment of words, can change everything. Geoff hadn't known this moment was going to come, he hadn't planned for it, he hadn't realised it would happen so soon. Words came and went and trembled on his lips. Words that could toss off the moment and alter it from an epiphany to nothing; or words that could make the earth shake and shatter.

He could say to Petra something like, 'Because I'm a sucker for tears' or 'Because you're so cute when you cry.' That would be easy enough, he was used to making light, flirtatious remarks that concealed what he was really feeling. Or he could be slightly more honest and tell her that he liked her, that she was nice herself, that he admired her. Even that would be easy, because he had in the past been more honest with Petra than any other woman he'd known. Or he could tell her the truth, and that wasn't easy at all. It meant baring his own soul, it meant leaving himself wide open to rejection, and it meant laying the burden of his love on top of all the other burdens she was carrying. He supposed a saint would have been able to hold himself back from temptation and sacrifice his own emotions for someone else's, but Geoff was no saint. He was a man whose desire for Petra was so great that holding it in took every ounce of control that he possessed. Just having her in his arms was difficult enough. The fresh scent of her hair was close to driving him out of his mind.

'Sorry,' she said awkwardly, embarrassed at his silence and believing that she'd overstepped the bounds of friendship. 'That was a dumb thing to ask.'

'No,' he said, and the courage suddenly came to him, from where he would never know. 'It wasn't dumb at all. You see, I've ... I love you.' And he finally succumbed to his overwhelming need to touch her, to have her, to take her. With those words, he pulled her up close to him, lowered his head and, on soft lips that had parted with shock and surprise, kissed her with a passion he'd never felt before.

If she hadn't been so tired, so shaky, or so vulnerable, Petra might have been able to stop Geoff and to stop herself, but with her every defence down and her sense of reality shrunken to this small, dark place under the sky, to Geoff's arms around her, to his mouth on hers, Petra knew nothing except the wanting of him. The outside world had disappeared for her; the house with its lit windows seemed to be a ship sailing past them in the night; all her tomorrows had vanished, leaving only this moment as the one that counted, as the one that would endure. So she returned his kiss with an equal passion, her hands touching his face, curling in the crisp hair at his temples, feeling the shape of his head under her palms. Then she was lost in his mouth, in tongues that met and stroked, in lips moving on hers, and she barely felt their slow descent to the ground or the softness of the grass beneath her back.

The baring of her breasts to the night air was a release; his mouth on her nipples the fulfilling of an overwhelming need. Their shedding of clothes was quick and frenzied, their hunger for one another so deep and so pervasive that nothing would satisfy it but skin against skin, heated and flushed and aroused. Geoff's mouth burned where it touched her, on her breasts, her stomach, her hip, the soft cleft between her legs. She parted before him, aching and desirous, her fingers clawing at his shoulders, wanting him there, in her, stroking the depths of her. But he didn't oblige her. He merely murmured, 'Babies,' and then satisfied her the next best way—with his tongue and silken fingers— When she had finally stopped shuddering, she found him lying astride her, kissing her neck, her eyes, her temples. 'Geoff,' she whispered, 'what about you? Will you let me . . .?'

'Anything,' he said, his voice rough, his breath coming short and fast, 'anything you want.'

And, grateful to that detested lover who had, at least, taught her something about technique, Petra did to Geoff what he had done for her. Taking him in her mouth and hand, she caressed him until he arched towards the sky and his fist clenched spasmodically in her hair. When he was done, she lay very still, her head resting on his abdomen, the hairs of his belly crisp against her cheek, her hand resting on his chest, feeling his breathing slowly ease to normal.

'Wow,' he finally said. 'Thank you.' And he tugged on her hair.

'Thank *you*.'

Geoff laughed. 'Aren't we polite.'

'Bed etiquette.'

'My goodness, Petra, you sound like you've been in thousands.'

Petra shook her head gently, its weight bouncing a bit on the muscles of his stomach. 'Just one.'

'Whose?'

'A friend of a friend. Remember you once asked me if I'd had an affair that went sour? Well, that was it.'

'What went wrong?'

Petra dug her fingers into the hair on his chest. 'A combination of things. I really didn't like him and just wanted to lose my virginity. I was curious and he was possessive. Stuff like that.'

Geoff's voice was pensive. 'It sounds ugly.'

'It was, particularly at the end.' Petra shuddered a bit when she remembered the angry words that were exchanged and the nasty cracks that had been spoken.

There was a short silence between them, and Petra felt a warm breeze flow over her naked body. It was odd how comfortable she was. The softness of the grass took away from the hardness of the ground, and Geoff had curled up slightly so that one of his hands was idly rubbing her back. The sounds of crickets provided a steady chorus in the background, and the fireflies were now out in force, signalling to one another in tiny bursts of light. Petra felt as if she could stay in this spot for the whole night, for the rest of her life, for eternity.

'Geoff?'

'Mmmmm.'

'About what you said before.'

He immediately stiffened; she could feel his abdominal muscles tighten under her head. 'Petra, I . . .'

She pulled herself upright and clasped her arms before her breasts. Geoff was still stretched out before her, his length as white as the marble of a statue under the moon's unblinking illumination. 'No one has ever . . .'

'Petra, promise me something.'

'What?'

Now, Geoff was sitting up, too. 'Forget I ever said it.'

'But how can I . . .?'

'I can't talk about it. I'm sorry.'

Suddenly, it seemed as if they were strangers. 'But, Geoff, it's important. I just . . . how can I forget it?'

'You'll have to. Try to understand.'

'But I . . .'

'Please.'

The word was not a plea but a cold command, and she instinctively obeyed it, feeling the tears once again pricking at the back of her eyes. She wanted to tell him a million things—about the conflicting impulses in her heart, about her desire to put off decisions until after the swim, about how she had never wanted another man the way she wanted him, but he wasn't going to let her speak. He was standing up now, pulling on his shirt and then tugging on his briefs and slacks. Petra wanted to put her arms around him and tell him that she understood how vulnerable he felt after making that confession to her. Geoff was a man with too much pride to enjoy the fact that he'd fallen in love with a woman who couldn't say that she loved him in return. She wanted to say it, she longed to say it, but she couldn't. Petra was too confused to know what she was feeling.

Slowly, she stood up and put on her dress. It was crumpled and full of grass, and one of the buttons had come off in her haste to get undressed. When she was finished trying to brush it off and straighten the skirt,

Geoff handed her her bra and panties. She scrunched them up in her hand and then said in as casual a voice as she could manage, 'I'd hate your parents to see us like this.'

'They'll be in bed.'

But she couldn't feel casual about what had passed between them. There was an ache in her throat as she followed him across the grass and through the trees to the back patio of the house. The hands that she had used so often to stroke a willing cat or soothe an upset child wanted to touch him somewhere, anywhere, and ease the set rigidity of his shoulders, the fists clenched in his pockets, the jaw working in the side of his cheek. But for all their earlier intimacy, she knew she could not. He didn't want comforting or caressing, he wanted her to forget what she had said. *I love you.* No one had ever said that to Petra, not even her mother.

How could she say that she loved him, when she wasn't even sure what it meant—she who had spent so much of her life in a loveless condition? She didn't know what love signified to Geoff or how it made him feel. She was totally ignorant of love as an emotion or an act. Perhaps what she and Geoff had done together on the grass wasn't 'making love' at all. Perhaps it was merely a mutual easing of frustration and desire. Doubts began to assail her as they stepped into the house and made their way up the stairs and towards her bedroom. It suddenly occurred to Petra that Geoff didn't want to talk about loving her, because it had only meant something at the moment of speaking. His 'love' for her might have been an onrush of pity. God knows she'd asked for it. Or perhaps, the 'love' he felt was something that came and went. She knew how many lovers he'd had, he'd told her that. It was quite possible, she thought, with a painful twist of her heart, that he always said those words to a woman that he wanted.

They stopped before her bedroom door, and Geoff

was, politely, saying good night. Petra could tell that
the only thing he wanted was to get away from her, but
she couldn't help herself. She had spent a lifetime
starving for love, and now that it was so close to her,
she was still hungering, aching for it, needing it more
than she'd ever needed anything in her life.

'Geoff?' she whispered and reached out for him,
touching his arm with her outstretched fingers.

He had started to turn away, but now he stopped as
if her touch had burned him. 'What?' he asked coldly.

'Did you ... just tell me, did you mean it—that you
loved me?'

He looked at her long and hard, his features sharp
and chiselled under the angled hallway light. She saw
lines in his face that hadn't been there before, cut deep
between his mouth and nose, and she suddenly realised
that her asking was like a probe digging at an open and
hurting wound.

'Yes,' he said curtly. 'Goddamn it, yes.'

And, turning on his heel, he strode away, his limp
awkward and accentuated by his fatigue, his shoulders
bent as if he carried a burden almost too painful to
bear.

CHAPTER NINE

THE week before the swim was a hectic one. Joe had a
thousand details to attend to, many of which required
long-distance phone calls from Mercy to the firm that
was renting them the boats, to the company that was
supplying them with equipment, to those people who
had agreed to be on the team that would accompany
Petra across the lake. Sunny had to visit the hospital
once to have her stitches removed from her thumb and
one more time to have it checked by the surgeon. Petra
had thrown herself back into swimming as if it were the
only thing in the world that counted, and Geoff spent
several frustrating afternoons trying to write some
material for his article. He'd brought a small, portable
word-processor with him, but not even its speedy
editing software was any help with his writing.
Sentences were begun and discarded, paragraphs
eliminated with one stroke. All the fluency and skill
that Geoff had previously brought to his assignments
seemed to have evaporated into thin air.

He sat, one afternoon, in the shade of the porch,
typing in lines, deleting them and, knowing that his
efforts were hopeless, cursing under his breath. Down
below him, out in the middle of the lake, Petra was
swimming her umpteenth lap along with Joe who was
pacing her in a rowboat and Sunny who had gone along
to act as secretary. She was jotting down notes that Joe
barked to her on a clipboard of paper. Geoff wondered
briefly what was going on in Petra's mind as she swam
out there and then discarded the thought with the same
swift, sure strokes that he'd been discarding letters,
words and sentences. He couldn't afford to think about
Petra. Images and remembered sensations would come

flooding into his head and he would wince from the pain they would cause. He already knew what it was like. He'd spent two days after they'd come back to the cottage from his parents' house agonising about Petra. He was worn out from it, exhausted by it, and sick to death of his own misery and self-pity.

She didn't love him. That was clear enough to Geoff; she'd made that absolutely evident. She liked him, she liked his conversation, she liked his body, she liked his technique. He'd felt that way about a dozen women of his intimate acquaintance, and he could barely recall any of their names. Liking wasn't the same as loving. Geoff hadn't really understood the difference until he'd fallen for Petra so hard that he was shattered by the crash.

Loving her meant wanting her physically, needing to be with her, aching to share her life, fearing for her, exulting with her. Geoff had never felt that way about any woman before, and he was damned sorry for himself that Petra had awoken such emotions in him. Unrequited love, he was discovering, was hell. He wasn't eating, he hadn't been able to sleep well, he could barely keep a conversation alive and now he couldn't write either. It made him angry, frustrated and humble all at the same time. It made him far more repentant about the hearts he'd probably broken in the past and the women whose offers of love he'd spurned. At times he felt a compassion so deep for the sadnesses of the world that he wanted to cry and then, realising how maudlin he was becoming, he would grit his teeth, determined to pull himself out of this black hole if it was the last thing on earth he ever did.

And he castigated himself unmercifully for having let Petra know the state of his heart. He cursed the weakness that had let those three small words slip past his lips and out into the air where she could hear them. Geoff knew he was proud, too proud probably, but he couldn't help that pride. He didn't want Petra to feel sorry for him or to be kind to him out of pity. He'd felt that kindness welling in her as they lay naked on the grass, and he'd known he just couldn't bear it. His words about love had almost been forced out of him, but when they were out in the open, he hadn't wanted them dissected and analysed. He knew she was surprised, disbelieving and finally flattered, but he hadn't meant to pander to her ego. The words had come from the depths of his soul, and they were the sort of words that were incomplete by themselves. They were only the half of a whole, they demanded an answer. And the fact that Petra couldn't complete them, couldn't match them in kind had cut Geoff deeply. He had never expected that, when he finally fell in love with a woman, his feelings would be unreciprocated. Somewhere, inside himself, he'd been quite convinced that Petra would say—*Oh, but I love you, too. I always have*—or some other such romantic nonsense. What a fool he'd been, Geoff thought clenching his teeth, and the knowledge of his own idiocy flayed him.

Geoff tapped out a few words, thought about the ways in which the finished article would be syndicated across North America and tried to get excited about it. But thinking about his career made him more depressed than he already was. He'd once rated his work as the most valuable thing he possessed. Nothing in the world had seemed as important to him as the chance to travel, to interview the global movers and shakers, to be in the middle of events that would change the history of the world. But, like his writing ability, that feeling seemed to have evaporated, leaving him with a dull sense of having seen it all and no longer giving a damn.

A month before he would have sacrificed his other leg and an arm to be back in Beirut but now, if he were honest and faced the facts, Geoff would have to admit that the only place on earth that he wanted to be was with Petra. Some comedown for a war correspondent with an international byline and a reputation for being tough, restless and willing to take any risk that came his way. *What was that old axiom? Pride goeth before a fall?* Well, he'd been proud, arrogant and haughty. He'd thought women were irrelevant to his life and had used them as if they'd been discardable toys. He'd despised men who were married as conservative, sentimental and domesticated. The higher they are, the harder they fall. Geoff stared at the screen of his word processor and acknowledged his own weakness, his own vulnerability, his own need for love. He had thought he was unique, but he was no different from the rest of the human race. No different, at all.

Petra did her last training swim in her best time ever and came out of the water feeling more confident than she ever had. The lake, which loomed in her imagination like a black and endless expanse of water, took on a new dimension. She imagined herself entering its waters, swimming through its waves, and actually coming out the other side, walking on to the Canadian shore in a moment of triumph. She'd never actually allowed herself to think about the final miles; she'd concentrated on being in the right frame of mind for the start of the swim and developing techniques that would get her through the middle. The end, she suspected, might be the toughest part of all, when she was swimming with every resource depleted except for pure adrenalin.

She glanced up at the cottage and thought about packing for their departure early that evening. She was going back in her Toyota along with Rembrandt while Joe and Sunny would take Jennifer, Renoir and all the luggage. Geoff was taking off on his own after lunch. She wouldn't see him again until the swim which was two nights away. Because of the intensity of her training and the concentration now required of her, Petra had been forced to put thoughts of Geoff aside. His presence made her both miserable and ecstatic at the same time, and those two emotions battling within her threw her off her stride, caused her to falter when she should surge ahead and ruined the smooth regularity of her strokes. The one time she'd let thoughts of Geoff intrude on her training, she'd done so badly that Joe had practically torn his crew-cut out at the roots.

Petra stretched her arms upwards towards the sun, trying to ease the fatigue in her shoulders, and then sat down on her towel on the sand and watched Jennifer race the last lap into shore. Joe had been timing her as well and, although his look was gruff as he glared at the stopwatch, Petra knew that he was pleased with his racer's performance.

'Pretty good, isn't she?' Petra called out to him.

'Not bad,' he muttered and, as Jennifer came out of the water, he repeated it to her, 'Not bad, sweetheart. Not bad at all.'

Jennifer shook out her pigtails. 'Olympic time?' she asked.

'Close enough,' Joe said, 'but don't think you'll be giving up when we go back to Toronto. Two weeks' holiday and then I'll see you at the pool.'

Jennifer wrinkled her nose at him as he marched off and then came to sit down by Petra, flopping down on a towel and looking up at the sky with a pensive face. 'Sometimes, I wonder,' she said. 'I mean, it's really neat to think about winning a gold medal, but I don't know if it's worth it.'

Petra gave Jennifer a look of sympathy. She knew the feeling. 'It's a great achievement.'

'Yeah, but like, what's there afterwards? Just more school and college and . . . well, life.'

Petra restrained a smile. 'It would open doors to you. An Olympic medal will help you get into college and find jobs. People are impressed by the kind of determination and effort that goes into winning.'

Jennifer's brown eyes were bewildered. 'I guess so.'

'Anyway, you mustn't give up now. You're getting so close.'

'What are you going to do, Petra? After the swim, I mean?'

Petra shrugged and stared out at the lake. 'Go back to teaching.'

'Do you have any boy friends?'

Of all the people in the world that Petra could have a heart-to-heart with, Jennifer was the least likely. 'Nobody right now,' she said.

'What about Geoff?'

'Geoff?' Petra gave her full attention to Jennifer and wondered precisely what vibrations she'd managed to pick up through the smokescreen of emotion and ignorance that filled her adolescent mind. 'What about him?'

'I think he likes you.'

'We're friends.'

'I don't know.' Jennifer gave an envious sigh. 'If he looked at me the way he looks at you with those dreamy blue eyes, I swear I'd faint.'

'We're good friends,' Petra said carefully.

But Jennifer wasn't listening. 'He's like a movie star,' she said. 'Like Robert Redford, you know what I mean? I just wish I were older. I'd go after him in a minute. That's what my sister says, you know.'

Petra was giving Jennifer a look of fascination. 'No, I don't know. What does she say?'

'She says that there's no point in sitting around and waiting, that a lot of guys want the girl to do the running.'

'Really?'

'Uh-huh. I mean, if I had a choice between Geoff and an Olympic medal, I'd take Geoff any day of the week.'

'Jennifer,' Petra said severely, 'that's not the way to think. You mustn't imagine that you'd give up a goal like the Olympics for a . . . boy or a date. You have to achieve what you're capable of doing.'

Jennifer gave her the full benefit of a wide-eyed stare. 'You mean, that if you had the choice of marrying a man like Geoff or swimming the lake, you'd choose the lake?'

'Nobody has to make choices like that.'

But Jennifer was caught up in the delight of a romantic and melodramatic situation. She leaned towards Petra. 'But, what *would* you do?'

'Jennifer, this conversation is silly, really it is.' Petra stood up and shook out her towel. 'Besides, we'd better go back to the cottage. We both have a lot of packing to do.'

Jennifer stood up reluctantly. 'I hate packing.'

'I'll tell you what,' Petra said. 'I'll help you pack as long as you make me one promise.

'What's that?'

'No more talk about quitting—even if Robert Redford comes marching into your life.'

Jennifer gave Petra a small, dimpled smile. 'I guess I shouldn't hold my breath, right?'

'Right.'

But later that evening, as she was driving away from the cottage, the conversation with Jennifer came back into Petra's mind. She knew what Geoff was feeling, but she had tried not to think about it, tried to keep the memories of that night from flooding in on her. But she couldn't always stop them from coming, and they gave a bouyancy to her step and a pink glow to her cheeks. He loved her and the knowledge of that love delighted her beyond anything she'd ever known. She'd spent so many years believing that she was unlikable and unlovable that the knowledge of his feeling for her was like a warm rain falling on the parched desert of her soul. Love wasn't a commodity that Petra had ever thought to possess.

But that knowledge wasn't enough to keep her from feeling, at the same time, deeply unhappy. She knew Geoff was miserable; she could see it in his face, the way he spoke, the extra-awkward limp that afflicted his walk. Her heart went out to him, but even that sympathy could not make her speak. Petra was excited by Geoff and thrilled by the fact that he wanted her, but she simply didn't know if she loved him in return. She didn't know what love was; she couldn't see it, touch it or measure it. She felt like a blind man in the world of the sighted, crippled by her ignorance and her past. One night, just before going to sleep, she had said to herself, 'I love you,' trying out the words, tasting them on her tongue, feeling their roundness in her mouth. But they had felt odd and awkward, and she had realised that she couldn't say them with sincerity and honesty.

But, if nothing else, she was utterly thankful to Geoff that he had been there when she needed him, strong, supportive and understanding. She didn't know how she could have handled her mother's death alone; until the funeral she hadn't realised how she felt about Sheila. For years, she had simply coped with her mother's illness, her emotions buried under a vast weariness by the demands it made on her. It wasn't until Petra had watched the coffin being lowered into the ground that all the feelings she'd held at arm's length for so long—sadness, anger, frustration, hatred, relief, guilt, grief—had come rushing in upon her in a vast, tumultuous wave. She couldn't deal with them; she didn't know what they meant and she was afraid of the way they battered at her. Crying had helped a bit, but she'd had to talk them out. And Geoff hadn't been shocked by the violence and ugliness of her confession. He hadn't chastised her for not loving her mother enough, for not being loyal, for being relieved at her death. He'd merely held her in his arms, his presence enormously comforting and reassuring.

Petra manoeuvred the car off the rutted, dirt road and out on to the highway, the Toyota seeming to give a sigh of relief as its springs stopped bouncing.

'Okay, Remmie?' she asked, looking into the back seat.

The dog just lifted his head and then put it back down. When it came to long car rides, Rembrandt liked to pass the time snoozing. He'd taken one look at the bags Petra had put in the boot and then settled in for a solid nap.

Petra looked back at the road and tightened her hands on the wheel. Somehow, in her mind, thoughts of Geoff and the swim were all entangled together. When she thought about loving him and wondering what that would mean or feel, she found that she couldn't look beyond the distance of next week and the thirty-two miles in the water and the sixteen or seventeen hours of swimming. It was as if any emotion that she might have was not only buried beneath the weight of that obligation, but also waiting to reveal itself at the end. Jennifer's words came back to her. What would she do if she were given the choice of marrying Geoff or swimming the lake? Petra didn't put the question to herself in such simplistic terms. What was the greater goal, she thought, learning to love Geoff or crossing the lake? Were they separate goals or were they one and the same? Petra couldn't sort it out in her head. All she knew was that in some mysterious way, her feelings about Geoff and the swim were linked together, and the meaning of that connection would not be made clear until it was over.

'Psst? Sunny? Are you asleep?'

The mattress on the bed rustled as Sunny shifted position. 'No,' she said, 'how can I be asleep when you're trying to keep me awake?'

'I don't like it,' Joe said. 'I just don't like it.'

'Shhh—you're going to wake everyone up.'

'I've got that uneasy feeling.'

'For heaven's sake, what uneasy feeling?'

'This feeling I have.'

'Now, Joe, since when can I read minds? Especially yours. You've been a mystery to me for thirty-five years.'

'Sunny, it's Petra. I'm worried about Petra.'

'Tch—last time I heard, she was doing great.'

'It's not her physical condition.'

'Then what is it?'

'It's her mental state.'

'She seems ready, Joe. She seems very confident.'

'It's Geoff.'

'Geoff!'

'There's something going on there, and it's affecting her mental state. I can tell.'

'Well, of course, there's something going on there. You'd have to be blind, deaf and dumb not to notice.'

There was a furious rustle of sheets and blankets. 'All right, Sunny, what are you trying to say? Spill the beans.'

'They're lovers.'

Pause. 'Lovers! Petra and Geoff? Did she tell you that?'

'Of course not.'

'Well, then—how do you know?'

'I can tell, that's how. You should see the way he looks at her, and the way she looks back at him. Heavens, Joe, it's as obvious as the nose on your face.'

Sigh. 'Damn it. Double damn it.'

'Now, Joe, it's good for Petra. She needs a man in her life. Of course, I'm not saying the path of true love is going smooth for her. I sense some tension there, but I think he's crazy about her. You know I wasn't sure a couple of weeks ago that Geoff was the right man for her. I didn't trust him. But now I think she's got him wound up good and tight. He doesn't know what's hit him.'

'He's not doing her swimming any good, I can tell you that.'

'Oh, come on, Joe, you're imagining things.'

'The hell I am. She loses her concentration now and then.'

'Swimming isn't everything, you know.'

There was a short silence and then, 'Blasphemy, woman. I've never heard such blasphemy.'

'Petra needs a man as much as she needs to get across a lake. She's just blossoming, can't you tell?'

'No, I can't. What I can tell is that I've got a swimmer on my hands who might not go the distance because her brain's all mushed up with thoughts of hearts and flowers.'

'Well, Joe McGinnis, is *that* what you call it?' Sunny asked, and then there were sounds that, to a discerning ear, might have suggested a small affectionate scuffle and several exchanged kisses.

Finally, when the sounds subsided, Joe's whisper once again filled the small bedroom. 'Still,' he said, his voice unhappy, 'I'm worried about her. It's going to take everything she's got to make it. And every time I get a swimmer who's in the midst of a love affair, I get problems.'

'You can't begrudge Petra some romance, can you?'

'Give a woman a little bit of romance and she can't keep her mind on anything.'

'You were pretty romantic once,' Sunny said slyly.

'Never.'

'Ah! Why, I can remember one afternoon in a park when . . .'

Joe gave a little laugh. 'Those were the days, weren't they, Sunny?'

She cuddled up to him and felt his arm pull her closer. 'Yes,' she said softly, 'they sure were.'

Geoff sat in one of the pace boats, a hot mug of coffee clenched between his hands, the wind from Lake Ontario lifting his hair. It was a south wind, the best kind Joe had told him, warm and gentle. The lake was at 71 degrees which had the swim team cheering with delight, and the surface of the water was as calm as it was ever going to get. Little ripples splashed against the edge of the boat, making small slapping sounds. Geoff was sharing a boat with Joe and they were part of a four-boat entourage that surrounded Petra as she swam. Geoff couldn't see the other boats very well, illumination by moon and stars only revealed them to him as shadows, but their lights threw beams on the blackness of the water and he could hear the hum of their motors and the occasional voices of their occupants.

The pilot boat, a 30-foot launch, was being run by a navigator who was keeping the swim on course to Toronto. They'd started on the opposite shore, the American side at Niagara-on-the-Lake, because a swim that was south to north followed the lake currents and the wind. The conditions were ideal, Joe had said with satisfaction when they started, and the weather forecast was good. But Geoff was well aware, as they all were, that the lake was unpredictable and the winds around it were erratic. A north wind could spring up seemingly from nowhere churning the small ripples into waves and causing the temperature of the water to plummet. But no one on the team talked about that—what they had discussed was the clarity of the night sky, only an occasional wisp of cloud passing over the moon, the warmth of the water, the benevolence of that lovely, south wind.

Although Geoff had known about the arrangements for the swim, he'd still been amazed when the equipment and all the members of the team had been assembled. In addition to the pilot boat, there were two pace boats and a boat behind. There was radar equipment, huge blankets, ropes, safety and first-aid equipment. And the team comprised a doctor and nurse, the navigator, the drivers of the other boats, two members of the Ontario Solo Swim Association who were to make sure that all regulations were being met,

Joe and another trainer, and several swimmers who were to pace Petra throughout the swim. The anticipated time of the swim was seventeen hours, and Petra would be swimming into daylight. At first, it had seemed odd to Geoff that lake crossings began at night, but now he could see the logic. No swimmer liked to swim at night, but a seventeen-hour crossing required some hours of darkness, and it was safer at night when the swimmer was fresh than when she was tired.

'Five miles,' Joe said, 'and she's going great.'

Geoff looked up from his cup of coffee to see that Joe was exactly where he'd been minutes before, standing at the side of the boat, his eyes glued to the water. Geoff followed his glance to where Petra was swimming. It wasn't hard to keep track of her. She wore a fluorescent tube on her back and one of the boats had an arc light beaming down on her. She was also wearing a light-coloured bathing suit so that her slender figure was visible against the back-drop of black waves. He couldn't see her face though—she was wearing two bathing caps and a huge pair of goggles. He could tell nothing about her except that she was swimming strongly, her pace steady and confident.

He looked back behind them and saw that the American shore had disappeared over the horizon, its lights no longer winking at them. For the first time, it came to Geoff just how isolated they were, out in the middle of Lake Ontario with eighty fathoms of water beneath them, miles of water around them and the vast dome of black sky above them. Their only lifelines were the ship-to-shore radios, slender threads connecting them to the Canadian shore.

'Yeah,' he said, 'she's looking good.'

'And the best conditions for a swim I've ever seen,' Joe went on, rubbing his hands together in triumph. 'It's like a bathtub out there. I can't see any reason why she won't make it nice and easy. She's mentally psyched for it and in the best physical shape of her life. A piece of cake, that's what I say, a goddamn piece of cake.'

'But her training sessions have only been for twenty miles and the lake crossing is almost double that. Won't she get tired?'

'Tired? Oh, sure, she will, but that's where my job comes in. I'll talk her in to shore, don't worry.'

But Geoff wasn't worried about the swim, which as Joe had said seemed to be a piece of cake, he was worried about other things, none of which he could voice to Joe or anyone else, so he sat hunched up in his seat, the coffee slowly cooling in his hands, his eyes watching that small, beloved figure.

'Tea break.'

Petra stopped swimming at the tap on her shoulder. Through the blurred plastic of her goggles, she could see the face of Don, one of the swimmers who would pace her. 'What?' she yelled. Her ear plugs blocked out almost every sound.

'Tea!' He gestured towards Joe's boat and she saw the pole coming at her with the plastic cup dangling from the hook at its end. In it would a mixture of strong tea and honey, her only form of sustenance during her swim. She didn't feel thirsty, but Petra knew that her body was using up fluid at a rapid rate and, if she didn't drink regularly, she'd become dehydrated. Treading water, she reached for the cup and drank deeply, inhaling its steam and feeling the tea's warmth flow inside her.

'How're you feeling?' Don yelled.

'Great.' She gave him a V-for-victory sign with her fingers.

'You're on hour six.'

She'd thought as much. It must be getting close to five in the morning, because the first glimmers of daylight were showing in the sky to the east, lightening the sky and dimming the stars. She looked forward to daylight. Although she was feeling wonderful, Petra didn't like swimming in the dark. Too much darkness, too much the feeling that she could slip below those black waves into some endless night and never emerge into the light again.

'I'm going to be staying with you for awhile,' Don said.

'How come you're so lucky?'

'That's the breaks,' he said, and she could just make out his grin in the darkness.

Petra let the cup go, waved at Joe and then started out again. She could sense Don swimming alongside her and matched herself to his strokes. *One and two and three and four and . . .* the rhythm set again, she slowly forgot his presence and never even felt him leave her after a mile had passed. She had once again fallen into an oblivion where she saw nothing, heard nothing and felt nothing, her arms and legs moving automatically, her mind slipping into the warm and soothing place.

The first sign that the second half of the swim was going to be far different from the first half occurred at around 9:30 that morning when a dark bank of clouds appeared on the northern horizon. At first, they merely looked like land when seen from miles away, but it was soon apparent to everyone that they were far less innocent. A cold breeze sprang up, and the lake turned choppy with one small wave crashing into another, sending little plumes of spray into the air. Petra forged ahead in it, seemingly oblivious of the changes, but two of the pace swimmers came out, shaking their heads and saying that it was getting tough. Joe began to check the water temperature every half-hour but the drop in temperature was minuscule, and he'd scowl at the thermometer and then breathe a sigh of relief. 'It's okay,' he'd say to Geoff. 'This shouldn't bother her in the least.'

By 10:30, the bank of clouds had grown to a mass

that covered the sun, casting a shadow miles wide which darkened as the day went on. Geoff had to remove his sunglasses which had protected his eyes from the reflection of sunlight on water, because he could no longer see well enough through them. Like everyone else in the four boats, his worried glance was on Petra. She hadn't faltered yet in the regularity of her strokes, but she had slowed down as the water grew even choppier. When she was stopped for another drink and asked if she was tired or cold, she merely shook her head. Joe had said, 'That's a girl,' but Geoff had felt his heart tighten. He watched Petra grab the cup of tea, drink it down and then start swimming again. What he sensed was that she hadn't spoken because she couldn't, because she had no energy left to utter even a word. He hunched down at the side of the boat and zipped up his slicker against the increasing strength of the wind. For the first time since the crossing began, he was now swimming with Petra, feeling each stroke in his arms, feeling each kick in his legs, feeling the onset of fear.

Waves battered and buffeted her; water filled her mouth occasionally when she opened it to breathe. Time and time again, Petra was rudely dragged out of her meditative state to confront the fact that the swim was getting harder and harder, that her muscles were protesting against the increasing coldness of the water, and that it was taking more and more energy to swim. For hours, she had merely glided through the water, now she was fighting it to maintain her balance, her course and the need to take an unimpeded breath. Like some large dormant animal, the lake had rested quietly, but now that it was aroused, it had turned angry, jumping out at her, hitting her with cold slaps. Spray filmed her goggles, and she choked once as water forced itself up her nose. She stopped swimming for a second and vaguely heard the yelling from the boats before starting off again. *Easy*, she said to herself, *easy, Petra*.

And she sang to herself, Christmas carols, the little songs she taught her grade three children, the few pop hits that she knew, folk songs from the sixties. *I want to teach the world to sing in perfect harmony* . . . Arm over arm. Up, around and over. Legs on a steady beat. Kick. Kick. Kick.

At 1:45 the rain began. At first it fell lightly, a mist over the lake, but soon it was a steady downpour, the drops making little circles on the waves, and a pattering sound on the decks of the boats. All the members of the team had pulled hoods over their heads, their edges framing faces that looked on with worry, concern and dismay. The temperature stabilised and grew no colder, but Joe was now taking the temperature of the water every fifteen minutes and muttering to himself constantly. 'Not so bad,' he'd say, or, 'It could be worse,' or, 'Come on, give us a break now.' Geoff didn't know what deity Joe was talking to, each of them had his own private god to bargain with at times like this. Geoff himself was praying that Petra would simply manage to get through the crossing. He knew how much it meant to her; he knew that if she had to quit, she'd force herself to try again. And he sensed that nothing in her life would move forward until this goal was achieved. She was too stubborn to give up it up on one try. Far too stubborn.

She was caught in a nightmare, a dark and damp nightmare that didn't want to quit. Cold rain beat down on her back, water poured in her mouth, every time she opened her eyes she saw a greyness around her. She no longer knew whether it was morning, afternoon or night. She no longer knew how long she'd been swimming. Every ounce of her concentration was focused on her arms and legs. They felt like lead weights that she could move only in the slowest of motions. *Up* . . . *around* . . . *and over. Kick, one, two* . . . *kick, one, two, three* . . . *kick* . . . *try to kick.*

She wondered in her few moments of clarity why she had ever thought it possible to swim Lake Ontario. What arrogance had possessed her? What hubris had made her think she could conquer the lake? She was nothing in this vast expanse of wave and spray, nothing but a speck, a small and struggling speck—a piece of debris tossed on the back of an angry lake. And why was she doing it? What was she aiming for really—a thin segment of land on the empty horizon? Or something else? Something far different. *Swim, push, kick, pull—again and again and again.* Her body was numb from the cold, from the effort of moving. The ache had subsided, but Petra knew that the numbness was only the forerunner of something far worse. When it wore off, she would be in agony. *If I only knew why,* she thought helplessly. *If I only knew why.*

By 3:30 the rain had angled sharply as the wind picked up again. All around them was a heavy fog, and the small entourage of boats and swimmer seemed to be in a world of their own, walled in by the grey mass of air on every side. Joe was pacing the small length of the boat, cursing, muttering, and hitting one opened palm with a tightly clenched fist. Geoff was crouched on a seat, unable to take his eyes off that tiny figure in the water. Occasionally a gust of wind would blow the rain into his eyes and he wouldn't be able to see Petra, or a wave larger than the others would splash over her, concealing her beneath its foam. Then he'd jerk upright, his heart in his throat, its pounding so loud that he couldn't hear anything but the sound of his own terror.

A shout caught his attention, and he saw Joe picking up the megaphone.

'What!'

The radio operator in the lead boat was standing at its stern end and hollering through his hands. 'Land! Two miles to land!'

Joe dropped the megaphone and turned to Geoff in

triumph. 'Two miles. She's going to make it.' He laughed and threw his arms out wide. 'Goddamn it, but she's going to make it!'

Those in the other boats had also heard the news and Geoff could hear a faint cheering and see fingers raised in victory signs, but somehow he couldn't share the joy around him. Those final two miles were going to be the worst in Petra's life, he could tell by the way she was stroking, by the slow turning of her head, by that tired kicking. He felt her exhaustion deep within him, his arms and legs bone-weary, his head aching with the effort to keep going.

One of the pace swimmers dropped into the water and swam to Petra to tell her the good news, but no one was sure that she caught his words, because she seemed not to notice that he was there. Doggedly, she just kept on swimming.

In the nightmare, in the horrible, unending nightmare, there was a distant shore. Just as she was close to it, the shore would recede, slipping away from her, falling back into the line of the horizon, a darker grey shadow disappearing into a lighter one. Like love, it had no substance. She couldn't touch it; she couldn't get close to it. Try as hard as she might, Petra couldn't reach it. *Love is a distant shore*, she thought tiredly, *too far away for me*. All her life she had been swimming towards it, running towards it, trying to find it, but she couldn't. It had never been there for her. What arrogance had ever led her to believe that she would be one of the lucky ones? She couldn't reciprocate the feelings of the man who loved her. The love she felt for her mother, buried beneath layers of sadness and anger, had not even been able to rise to the surface at her death. Petra tried to understand why she was here, in this nightmare, trying so hard to reach that distant shore, but she no longer could find any reason for it. The shore was a mirage, that's all, an illusion, a fake.

Without even being quite aware of what she was doing, Petra stopped swimming. She came upright so that the rain beat directly into her goggles, and she couldn't see anything around her, not even the boats on all sides or the grey mass of sky and water. Taking a deep breath, she tore off her goggles and threw them away, pulled out her ear plugs, and wrenched the caps off her head. Like a living thing, the water grabbed each item as it fell, tossed it into the air, pulled it to and fro and then sucked it into the depths. Within seconds, there was no sign of any of them.

'Petra! Petra!' Joe was screaming through the megaphone. 'There's only two miles to go! Toronto is two miles away!'

Geoff's hands were clenched on the side of the boat. 'She's too cold, Joe. She can't go on.'

'The temperature is at 65,' Joe barked at him. 'That's not too cold. If it went below that I'd pull her out in a minute.' He lifted the megaphone again. 'Come on, Petra! Don't give up now!'

And Geoff could hear the others yelling encouragement at her.

'Two miles, Petra!'

'Go for it!'

'Come on, sweetheart!'

She seemed dazed, uncertain. Slowly she swivelled in the water, turning in 360 degrees as if she were lost, as if she were trying to locate the whereabouts of those voices. It was Geoff who finally figured out what was the matter.

'She's crying,' he said, and his stomach tightened as if a fist had slammed into it. 'Joe, for Christ's sake, she's crying.'

'She can't give up now,' Joe snapped at him. 'She'll hate herself later. Hell, she'll want to kill me if I stop her.'

'She doesn't want to swim anymore.'

'The hell she doesn't. She's just tired and confused.'

He turned to one of the pace swimmers who shared the boat with him. 'Get her more tea, Bob. Let's give her some energy.'

Was he the only one of them that could see her face? Geoff thought in desperation. She was crying out there, her eyes squeezed shut, her mouth open and trembling. 'Joe! Pull her in!'

Joe was like a bantam rooster as he faced Geoff with his hands on his hips, his feet planted wide apart, his eyes narrowed. 'She stays.'

'Goddamn it! You're torturing her!'

'She knew it wouldn't be easy.'

'She's crying. Crying!'

'Lots of swimmers cry.'

Geoff glanced from Joe's adamant expression to Petra's agony, and the decision came to him, the knowledge of what he had to do. With one flick of his wrist he had unzipped his slicker. He threw it off and stripped the buttons from his shirt in his haste. When his torso was bare, his jeans went next, his back bare and wet in the rain, his hair turning dark as it dampened. He tore off his briefs, his sneakers and socks. Before Joe really realised what he was going to do, Geoff was over the side of the boat, a naked body in diver's arch as it hit the water and went under.

The water pulled him down in its cold grasp, and his body went rigid as it plummeted into the blackness. He had to claw his way to its surface, fighting for air as he came to the top and choking when a wave slapped him in the face, filling his open mouth with water. When his eyes cleared, he swam towards Petra, ignoring the voices above him, the megaphone barking.

'Geoff! Get back here! Leave her alone!'

She was still crying when he approached her, treading water frantically and crying, her hair plastered to her head, the tears mixing with rain on her face. She looked so awful that Geoff wanted to take her in his arms and hold her tight, but he knew he couldn't offer her that sort of comfort.

He got within two feet of her and said in a voice loud enough to carry over the sound of wind and rain, 'Petra! Petra, it's me!'

For a second he didn't think he was going to get through to her, but then she blinked. 'Geoff?'

'Petra, I'm going to swim with you,' he said. 'We're going to make it together.'

She stared at him. 'You?'

'If I can do it, you can.'

'But . . . why?'

There was a gust of wind, and cold water splashed against his face. Geoff spat out a mouthful and then said, 'Because I believe in it. Because the swim is important.'

'You . . . you thought it was a waste of time.'

The megaphone was screaming obscenities at him, but Geoff ignored them. 'I was wrong about that. Remember that story my mother told us about her father and the way Marilyn Bell's swim gave him the will to go on? Well, I started to understand then what a swim like this means to people. It's not a waste; it's inspiring, it's courageous. Petra, I want you to make it. I don't want you to give up now.' And he meant it. Geoff had once thought her goal was an individual act, a selfish act, but as he had watched her struggle against the rain and the wind and the cold water, her swim had come to symbolise something else for him—it mirrored in a public way every private, lonely struggle, every human effort to overcome adversity, even his own fight for health.

The rain was beating down on her head, the drops running down her face so that he couldn't tell if she were still crying or not. 'Oh, Geoff,' she said shakily.

'So—I'd be honoured if I could come with you. Will you let me?'

'But . . . your leg? What if . . .?'

Even though he was freezing, even though the wind blew rain across his face, even though he wasn't sure he could swim two miles without dying, Geoff gave her one of his most charming and rakish grins. 'You'll just have to save me, Petra. Like you did the last time.'

'You're crazy.'

'No crazier than you.'

'Oh, Geoff,' she said again, but he realised that he was going to win for she was smiling at him, a trembling awkward smile, but a smile all the same.

'Good,' he said. 'So how about it? Let's hit the road.' Turning on his stomach, he began to swim and then realised that she still wasn't with him. He stopped, looked back and realised that she was crying again. 'Now, what's the matter?' he yelled.

She just shook her head as if she couldn't speak.

Geoff glanced up at the bobbing boats and realised with a sense of relief that the megaphone had stopped screaming at him. But everyone was watching, their faces tense and anxious. The rain had eased to a drizzle, but the wind had grown stronger so that the drops felt like needles on his skin.

'Come on,' he hollered. 'I'm getting wet.'

'Geoff?' Her voice wavered but managed to reach him.

'Yes!'

'I love you! I think I do!'

For a second, Geoff closed his eyes, afraid that his hearing had deceived him, afraid that what he had heard was a figment of his imagination. But when he opened them again, she was still there, and he felt a surge of joy within, an incredible burst of happiness that warmed him so completely that he forgot the dark cold of the water and the fury of the lake.

'I love you, too! Petra, I love you!'

Her eyes were huge and dark in the pinched whiteness of her face, but she was smiling when he reached her. 'I'm so sorry,' she whispered as he put his arms around her. 'But I didn't know. Oh, Geoff, I was so dumb.'

'It's okay,' he murmured, pulling her close to him. 'It doesn't matter.'

They tried to embrace; they tried to kiss, but the lake was stronger than their need for one another. It sucked them in the moment they stopped kicking or moving their arms, and they were forced to part so that they wouldn't go under. All they could do was face one another.

Petra had started to laugh. 'We pick the strangest places to make love.'

'Just wait until later,' Geoff said grimly. 'I'll get you then.'

Then the noise came to them; the cheering, clapping and whistling from the boats, and they both looked up, having forgotten that they were on a stage so to speak, with an audience watching their every move.

'Jesus Christ!' a scratchy voice squawked at them through the megaphone. 'Will you two lovebirds get a move on?'

Geoff gave Joe a military salute. 'Yes, sir,' he called and then looked towards Petra. 'Ready?'

'Yes,' she said. 'I'm ready.' And they both knew that they weren't talking about the swim or the two miles or that distant shore, but whatever life would bring to them together—marriage, children, changes that were unknown but no longer frightening or unwanted.

'Okay,' he said. 'Let's go.'

NEWS RELEASE:
(AP), August 7, 1984

'Schoolteacher Petra Morgan, 25, the latest woman to challenge Lake Ontario, finished her marathon swim in 19½ hours. While her time did not beat existing records, Miss Morgan demonstrated courage and endurance while battling rising winds, a changing current and rapidly dropping temperatures. For the last two miles of the swim, she was accompanied by her fiancé, journalist Geoffrey Hamilton, 36, who collapsed when they reached the shore and had to be rushed to the hospital where he was listed in fair condition due to severe exhaustion and hypothermia. Upon his release from the hospital, Mr Hamilton married Miss Morgan in a small, private ceremony in the home of her trainer, Joseph McGinnis. The couple will be taking up residence in Washington, DC, where Mr Hamilton has been posted as Washington correspondent for Allied Press, and Miss Morgan, retiring as a marathon swimmer, will join the teaching staff of Sidwell Friends Academy.'